An Account of
THERMOPYLAE
Leonidas, the Spartan King

Best Wishes

Alan Bristor

Alan Bristor

♠ **Right**
Bower
Interpretations

Right Bower Interpretations™
LURAY, VIRGINIA

Published by: Right Bower Interpretations™, Luray, VA
rightbower@hughes.net
www.etsy.com/shop/RightBower

Cover design: © 2016 Right Bower Interpretations™
The cover design pictures a Spartan shield with the *lambda* that represents the Greek letter "L". This letter on the shield signifies the area of Greece known as Lacedaemon. This is the region of Greece that encompassed Sparta.

An Account of THERMOPYLAE: Leonidas, the Spartan King
Alan Bristor -- 1st ed.

ISBN 978-0-9981395-0-0 (paperback)
ISBN 978-0-9981395-1-7 (eBook)
ISBN 978-0-9981395-2-4 (audio book)

Library of Congress Control Number: 2016954274

I stood before the phalanx, 60 men across and 10 lines deep. I looked at their faces. They were bruised, bloody but not beaten. These 600 men, led by Spartans, would face an attack from the unbelievable force now forming across from us. I addressed my brothers:

Today the Spartans will lead you into battle, but we are all Greeks, and this is a stand we are making for Greece. Your orders of the day: remain in the phalanx, never stop fighting!

— KING LEONIDAS

CONTENTS

PREFACE

This book came about due to my long-term interest in the subject of ancient Greek history. This interest and the knowledge gained of this subject dates back to my 1970's college days. However, this work came together in a different way and followed a different path in its development. In this book, King Leonidas converses with me, the author. This brings the reader into my semi-circle to receive the words as I received them. I chose to design this book as a conversational narrative as opposed to a traditional reporting of timelines and events. By doing this, you are brought beyond the history books and into the world of human conflict and emotion. I invite the reader to join me in my face-to-face conversations with one of the most prominent individuals of ancient Greece, King Leonidas. So, sit down, strap in, hang on tight, and experience the Battle of Thermopylae that occurred in 480 BC. This story, therefore, is a historical narrative written in the first-person perspective.

—Alan Bristor

PROLOGUE

Alan, I am Leonidas. You need not refer to me as *King*, for I am now simply, Leonidas. I can speak with you because you have the ability to *hear* and *see*. So, I am here to answer your questions. You called me. I know of you and your abilities.

I know that I will also have to speak in words that you will understand. I will take this a bit further. I will simplify my language and not impose words on you from the time when I existed in Greece. I will not ask you to understand terminologies used in the time period we are talking about. During this story, I also do not intend to speak of many of the other Greek coalition leaders by name. To clarify, I do not wish to complicate the story for you.

You asked about Thermopylae. You have explained that much work has been put forward to study that time in history. You have expressed that many historians and researchers have spent years and years sifting through data looking for clues trying to put historical facts together. Much of the information is very accurate.

You have also told me of the media that has been produced concerning the events at Thermopylae. I am honored by all those who have spent time studying, researching, and paying homage to the events of that time. I am further honored by the modern day attitudes of many toward the Spartans.

I have been witness historically to numerous events through time where few were asked to stand against many. The Spartans were not alone nor have they been alone in the pursuit of freedom.

I will speak from a different perspective. I will share my thoughts and my feelings concerning the events of those days.

So, the message that I offer up is one of humanity, in addition to, one of history.

This book is categorized as fiction. Some will understand the truth of this information I present. To others, it will be an interesting story of conflict and battle. I leave it to the reader to decide.

It is my story, in my words, speaking about the subject of Thermopylae through my eyes.

I will begin my story prior to going to Thermopylae.

CHAPTER ONE

THE DECISION TO FIGHT

The Greek Coalition

Life will flourish in Sparta as its king travels to his destiny on a field of honor.

I n the summer of 480 BC, the Spartans had agreed to participate as part of a coalition of Greek forces to defend *all* of Greece against an imminent Persian invasion. It was commonly known that King Xerxes of Persia had assembled the largest army of the time. This was different than preparing for any other campaign that the Spartans had been involved in prior to this point.

The decision had been made to mount our defense at a location in northern Greece. The reason Thermopylae was chosen was due to the limited accessibility of the area. The path that the Persians would have to follow to enter Greece would take them through the narrow Pass at Thermopylae.

This Pass was bordered on one side by mountains and on the other side by the Malian Gulf.

Because of a Spartan festival, we were unable to march our entire army to Thermopylae. You have to understand, in the day, we were a very religious people. Our worship was founded over a long period of time and we were, as you might say, set in our ways.

The coalition of city-states specifically requested that the Spartans lead them. It was also asked that I, King Leonidas, be in command of the entire coalition of forces.

I was honored at this on one hand, and on the other hand, not thrilled with the idea of going to Thermopylae with less than my full complement of Spartans. This could not be helped because of the festival.

The other complication was the *oracle*. The oracle made it clear that a king of Sparta would have to perish for Sparta to survive.

The *oracle of Delphi* refers to the place and the people where Greeks go to receive guidance. How it all works, I do not know. I do know that their information is specific and not usually general in nature. The oracles receive payment from anyone seeking information. They then provide a written answer to any requests.

The oracles are predictors of events and choices and sometimes offer up warnings. Once the information from the oracle is received, it is considered fact. It must be adhered to, followed, or acted upon.

You must understand that we did nothing without consulting the oracle; and furthermore, we did nothing without first checking a sacrifice of an animal. In your modern day, this would not be deemed an acceptable way to function. But, like I said, we were deeply steeped in our beliefs and our ways.

Oracles were sometimes questioned as to their validity. There were questions concerning the oracle I received relating to the predicted death of a Spartan king, but our beliefs prevented me from questioning it publicly.

The sacrifice had to occur concerning daily events, especially when in battle. I had a *reader* or *seer* named Megistias, but I call him Megis for short.

After receiving the oracle, I consulted Megis concerning the upcoming events. I killed a hen and left him to his work. After a short while, Megis turned to me and provided his reading. "Life will flourish in Sparta as its king travels to his destiny on a field of honor."

During the course of this story, I use abbreviations for many who I associate with, including my officers. Part of my reasoning is to not encumber this narration with a lot of hard-to-pronounce names. The other reason is that I like the abbreviated names that I have given these individuals.

This reader had the job of providing information he was able to gain by studying the sacrifice. It did not matter whether the sacrifice was a chicken or a goat. The reader's job was to present his reading to me. This reading was, in most cases, a predictor and could involve his knowledge of how the battle would go or how the trip would go. Essentially, whatever task was at hand, his reading would be directed to providing information concerning that task. The end result, I agreed to go to Thermopylae to lead the defense for Greece.

The logistics of this operation were horrendous compared to the organized and disciplined campaigns that were conducted by the Spartans alone. Agreements had been made by the Greek city-states. When the Spartans marched, the others would join in and follow us to Thermopylae. Until the actual event occurred, we had no idea how many soldiers each city-state would bring. Gathering the equipment and support necessary for a large campaign is mind boggling. The trip from Sparta to Thermopylae would take about a week and a half and would be complicated further by having to meet up with the soldiers who were going to be coming along.

Each Spartan soldier had a *helot* (personal servant) to assist him and to be responsible for making sure his armor, equipment, and personal needs were taken care of.

In present times, some view them as slaves of the Spartans. Although they were not Spartan citizens, they were, in fact, the workforce that provided all of our food and many of the services that are sometimes taken for granted during day-to-day living. The helots were largely farmers except for the ones who were employed by the citizen Spartans in their homes or to be in service to a Spartan soldier. It's because of the helots that we, as Spartans, were able to live a life as warriors.

There is no doubt why the city-states chose Sparta to lead. Sparta had a full-time army that trained diligently and was a mandatory part of every male citizen's life.

Although some look down on the helots, I looked at them as a *People* who served us with a pride and distinction; that in no way demeans their stature. On campaign, the helots not only served the soldiers but provided our meals and transported our supplies along with us.

My helot servant was to me a trusted individual who I felt comfortable confiding in. I knew, when in battle or in barracks, I could count on him to be there and provide my many needs.

As I sat thinking about the upcoming deployment, I took comfort in the fact that, at least, I will have my trusted helot servant Sari along to support me. Sari had been with me way before I became a king. I am in my fifties and I am sure Sari is twelve to fifteen years my senior. He has never shown anything other than loyalty and respect for me. His wrinkled face and short thin stature disguise his many abilities. He has a room in the Palace, so he can be available when I need a trusted soul.

To my knowledge, Sari has no known family. We first met when my first man-servant asked to leave me to be with ailing relatives. I chose Sari from a list of applicants wishing for this type of employment. He was very eager at his work and showed the instant ability to take care of details that made my life easier. It is a comforting thought to know he will be with me during this trying event.

So, when we went on campaign, there were probably three helots to each Spartan. Many helots were brought along and employed by the army to provide all the extras involved such as setting our camps, providing first-aid, clearing the battlefields, and carrying or transporting all the equipment.

In addition to the helots, the *perioikoi* are non-citizen residents who live in and around Sparta and in greater Lacedaemon (the larger area of the countryside that encompasses Sparta). The perioikoi are free people who provide all the other services and industry to Spartans.

The perioikoi collectively provide additional manpower in the form of soldiers when the Spartan Army goes on a campaign.

Although the perioikoi have other professions, they do practice soldiering under our guidance to help reinforce the number of troops that we can muster for any conflict.

CHAPTER TWO

CHOOSING THE "300"

The Spartan Captains

The sons of Sparta will lead the fathers of Greece in the battle for freedom. The scarlet cloak will dominate the field.

B ecause of the festival, I was only permitted to take three hundred men to Thermopylae with me. This is the number of men assigned to me as my *Personal Guard.* My normal Guard included a commanding officer and several other junior officers. The three hundred were totally at my disposal and were not subject to any rules or laws of Sparta. The Guard changed personnel from time-to-time. Although our laws dictate that I may have a Personal Guard of three hundred, there is no law stating who the three hundred must be.

This law caused much dissension among my soldiers. You must understand; we as a people were raised to be soldiers. To tell a soldier he cannot go fight because of a religious festival causes much concern, especially when the king must go.

To say that I was not apprehensive about our mission would be a lie. I knew whoever went with me would face the most serious fighting that they had ever encountered. I based this feeling on the understanding that the Spartans would be expected to lead and fight first. I had the rosters brought to me with the names of my Guardsmen.

As the time approached when I would have to leave for Thermopylae, I thought long hours on who to take with me. Attempts were made to influence my decision. I was receiving Spartan officers and soldiers daily, offering and in some instances, pleading to go. When men could not get in to see me, they would send dispatches with requests to be included in the Guard.

During this process of choosing my Guard, many of the leaders, or who you would call *generals*, came to me offering to go with my force. I declined these offers stating that I would be the general of my Guard.

I was overwhelmed with the support from the officers and men, but one thing I knew for certain, being a member of the current group of three hundred was no guarantee that they were going to Thermopylae. I needed a special group with me. My decision came to me in the night and it involved a meeting with my most trusted officers.

Before I asked Sari to summon my six officers for this meeting, I sent him to bring Megis for a reading. Megis arrived and we acquired a hen which I killed. Megis went to work and after a few moments offered his reading. "The sons of Sparta will lead the fathers of Greece in the battle for freedom. The scarlet cloak will dominate the field."

After my meeting with Megis, Sari had returned advising me that the officers had been summoned. These men are the ones who would help me with my terribly hard decision. The meeting was to be held in a large room of the palace.

I waited as the first of my officers entered the meeting room. Domesticles, who I call Dom, is short in stature and very muscular. He is a kind man who shows much compassion until you place a spear and shield in his hands. Dom then becomes a fierce warrior.

The next person to enter was Zenicetes. He is the commanding officer of the Guard at the present time. I refer to him simply as Zee. Zee is tall and is clearly focused on whatever subject is at hand. He has no humor and does not make light of things.

He is followed by Dienekes, his second-in-command. Dien is a soldier's soldier. He has dedicated his life to being a Spartan soldier. Dien has always pushed himself beyond what was expected of the rest of us. His determination and skill on the battlefield are second to none. He, like Zee, is a tall man.

Kronis and Gelon arrive together. Kronis is a huge man. I call him Kron. Gelon is an average-sized man and my closest confidant. He and I grew up together and attended the *Agoge* (State-sponsored school) in the same class. I was with him through the rigorous training that begins in our early youth and doesn't end until we are young adults. Both Kron and Gelon are currently assigned to other units of the Spartan Army.

We waited patiently for Illioneus to arrive. When he did, it was with much agitation. Illi is tall and thin, but very strong. He is also the youngest officer in our army. I came to know

Illi through his father. He was a fine captain who is now retired.

I intend to use the word *captain* as an identifier of Spartan officers. I do this because this is a term you will understand.

I looked at the group of men I had assembled. All wore close beards and long hair that grew past the shoulders and down the back. I know these six men better than any others. I trust these men over all others.

I explained that the reason Sari summoned them was to keep the purpose of our meeting confidential.

Kron commented, "Perhaps the King should have sent a soldier."

Without taking offense to his comment, I advised Kron, "Sari is as high on the list of people I trust as any of you!" I then looked at each face and asked, "Would each of you go to Thermopylae with me as part of my Guard?"

At this request, they all rose to their feet in a show of unity and support. I bid them, "Sit down."

"Before you decide, I want you to know that this will be different than any conflict we have fought in. The Spartans will be leading a combined force against a huge army. There are many questions about this deployment and few answers.

"I ask the six of you because I can count on you. The Guard is only three hundred men. I will command the Guard during this deployment. If you choose to go with me, each of you will officer fifty Spartans."

I studied their determined faces and said, "I need your verbal answer now."

Each man answered the same. "I am with you, Leonidas."

I told them, "I personally chose each of you and I wish for you to choose from either the Guard or active army, the fifty men you will command. My only stipulation is that no father and sons and no brothers be included. It is important to maintain each family line."

Zee then asked, "Have you any news or intelligence of the Persians?"

I said, "Not much. It is my understanding; they are in no hurry. It has also been reported that the Persian force is so massive that it takes days and days to gather together once they arrive at a location."

In his compassionate way, Dom asked, "Should we concentrate on volunteers?"

Dien said, "A volunteer is not necessarily the best soldier to take along."

Illi asked, "Should age play a part in our choices?"

Gelon said, "If age were to play a part, then why would we consider you?"

This drew a chuckle from the group, all except for Zee. The comment drew a smile from me.

I told Illi, "Age is not our concern. Just get the best you can find."

Dien said, "Just make sure they are all old enough to grow facial hair, Illi."

This brought another round of laughter; however, Zee once again remained straight-faced.

I looked at them and said, "Is everything clear?"

I received positive nods all around. I said, "Work quickly; we leave in days."

I dismissed my captains with the relief that they would bring our best fighters to Thermopylae. I trusted them and I wished for them to bring men that they, in turn, trusted.

Even though I had received what was considered to be an omen of death for myself, my men and captains did not view things this way. In their eyes, it was not a suicide mission.

There was one set of brothers who had insisted that if one went to battle with me, I must allow the other. This was done out of respect for their service in the Guard.

One other thing that should be noted; we did not view war the same as most. We were not adverse from having a good battle if we felt it was a *just* cause. We did not, as a People, go around haphazardly attacking other cities and countries just for the sake of it.

The Spartans went to battle with purpose. We also went to battle with the attitude that you either win or die trying. There was no middle ground. A Spartan does not understand the word *retreat*. With all this said, the Spartans still preferred to choose their battleground.

CHAPTER THREE

TO THERMOPYLAE

The Long March

*The lambda will dominate the land, and those who
follow the lambda will forever be honored.*

To prevent many of the city-states from being overrun, the collective Council agreed that Thermopylae was the absolute best place to form a defense to prevent the Persians from entering the main body of Greece. I agreed with them, so we were bound for Thermopylae.

Spartans could not leave their homeland without a good omen to travel on; so as was custom, I had my servant, Sari, get a sacrifice and bring me the reader. Sari arrived with a hen which I killed quickly. This was opened and given to our reader to study.

After a short time, our reader came back to me with his omen. "The lambda will dominate the land, and those who follow the lambda will forever be honored."

After the reading, I took a last look at the palace. I faced my wife and child. I looked into my son's eyes, putting my hands on his shoulders, and I said, "Be strong my son." I turned to my wife and held both of her hands in mine. Our eyes met. Without words, I crushed her to me in an intense embrace trying to swallow my emotion; nothing could be spoken. After our long silent embrace, I let go and left the palace.

I joined the assembled group and conducted an inspection. I went to the front after walking the full-length of combined manpower, carts, wagons, horses, livestock, and humanity, all gathered to go to war and to support that effort for as long as necessary. I completed this in about one hour only pausing briefly. The wagons and carts carried our food supplies. They carried replacement spears, shields, and armor. The extra equipment had two purposes: to replace equipment damaged or broken during battle and to provide equipment to those who joined us but were not properly supplied. The group getting ready to leave included our neighbors who had already joined up to march with us, as well as, our own perioikoi citizen-soldiers, several hundred helots and of course, the support wagons brought by our allies. This entire line of humanity and equipment would be following my Personal Guard.

Some supplies were brought along following the plan that the greater part of the Spartan Army would be joining us at the conclusion of the festival. Although the other city-states were providing soldiers and supplies, we had no hopes that they would provide anything beyond the support that came to Thermopylae during this initial deployment.

We began our march: Lacedaemonians that included the Spartans and their personal helots, followed by the perioikoi plus a few others, and the supply train. The soldiers marched without their heavy armor. They were dependent on their helots to take care of their equipment.

The march ahead of us would take many days. Our lines did ultimately become very spread out. The Spartans were used to marching at a rapid pace and getting to their destination and then resting. The others were not in this condition. The other troops required much more rest which slowed down the progress of our march. The Spartans were partly frustrated by this; however, it meant they would arrive at Thermopylae without needing a long recovery period.

When you're walking along, you think of many things. As the king, I had many thoughts of my own. They included my wife and child who I had left behind and what would become of them if I failed to return.

I took the responsibility of being king seriously. Although I was born into a royal family, I never expected or sought the title which I now bear. After considering things, maybe it was better this way. I had no preconceptions nor did I have any grand aspirations. I just simply wished to serve my country and be a good leader.

It dawned on me that everything that had happened in my life had led up to this moment and this event. It is as if my whole life were a preparation for this particular mission. This thought overwhelmed me.

When we took breaks, I did not sit with the troops. I needed to be by myself. I remained focused on my own thoughts. I felt a large obligation and responsibility to the soldiers and the people of Greece.

While sitting alone during one of our many breaks, I was visited by Dien, one of my captains. Dien wanted to talk about the upcoming battle, but I wanted to reflect on everything that brought us to this moment. I felt bad in putting him off, but I needed this time alone.

My servant, Sari, brought me water which I thanked him for, but, I then also told him that I wished to be alone.

I knew that, in the coming days when we got to Thermopylae, I would not have any time alone. I wondered if the way of life of Sparta would be able to continue if we failed. During this march, I repeated this process of being alone often. When we would camp for the night, however, my Guard would not allow me to be too far away from their protection.

Each day of travel increased the numbers of our coalition. As we passed from city-state to city-state, the troops promised were delivered. They joined the rear of our formation creating miles of soldiers, carts, livestock for food, and all the equipment and supplies.

It was agreed, that if we remain at Thermopylae long, the coalition of city-states would support our efforts with resupplying our needs. But for now, we were taking everything with us that we needed.

Mile after mile we marched in a relaxed formation with the Spartans in the lead, followed by their helot servants, keeping their equipment close at hand. The perioikoi were next followed by the massive supply train for all the Lacedaemonians.

As we approached a city-state, the Spartans would halt allowing their helot servants to bring up their helmets and shields and war-cloaks. It was important for the Spartans to appear as if they were ready for battle when they went through each city-state. After passing through a city-state, they would, once again remove their heavy equipment and allow their servants to carry it.

The city-states did show us honor by turning out and watching the Spartans and the rest of the soldiers march by. When the Spartans passed through, there was no doubt that people were witnessing professional soldiers. The Spartans marched in a disciplined manner carrying their spears, shields, and helmets with red horse-hair crests. The long flowing scarlet war-cloaks presented an appearance that made us look bigger than life. During this campaign, I had insisted that all Spartan troops wear red-crested helmets. This was to include me and my officers. We did attract much attention and awe as we marched through the villages and cities along the way.

It was my idea to allow the helots to carry the burden through the countryside, so as to preserve the strength of the Spartans for fighting.

Since we were camping with not only the Spartans, and we were gradually picking up more soldiers from other city-states, my officers felt it was important to protect their king. So, I did not interfere with the captains' orders to guard my personal camp.

Although it was felt that I could trust any Spartan soldier and perioikoi and most helots, the other soldiers were not as well-known to us and for all we knew, could have been infiltrated with Persian spies or assassins. So, I did not object to the precautions taken by my comrades.

We would begin each day with a sacrifice and a reading of that sacrifice. This was done before anyone could march. The omens were good in the early sacrifices on our way to Thermopylae.

Many of the city-states, who were allies of Sparta, had received training from Sparta concerning military tactics. As king, I felt it important to embrace our allies as future protection for our own area of the country. The roads leading to Thermopylae were not grand affairs. They were rough roads which caused further delays in our travel.

On one evening, when we camped, I called together the leaders of the various forces who were accompanying us so far. As I sat around a fire, I looked at the faces of the men who would be leading our allied troops. These men were politicians or high-ranking citizens of their city-states. Most were not soldiers. They wanted to know how I felt about things, but I knew what they really wanted to know. They wanted to know if I felt we could win at Thermopylae. These men were leading farmers, cobblers, and assorted other workers. They were not experienced with this type of warfare.

The closer we drew to Thermopylae, the more apprehensive they became. The leaders needed something from me. It was my job to deliver that something, and in this case, that "something" had to be hope.

I knew when our meeting broke up, that they would go back to their troops and report what I told them, so I chose my words carefully. I told them, as a military leader, I felt Thermopylae was the absolute best place in Greece to stop the Persians. If they did what I asked them to do, and if they followed the example of the Spartans, we could win.

I don't know what effect my words had on these volunteer leaders, but I gave them everything I could to give them that hope.

The journey to Thermopylae seemed longer than it should have been. It seemed as though we were always taking breaks waiting for our supplies and allies to catch up. The Spartans and perioikoi marched well, but we had gotten so strung out that the end of the line was a full day behind the rest of us, so we waited.

My thoughts, as we drew closer, drifted from Sparta to Thermopylae. I had never been to Thermopylae, but it had been described to me. It sounded like a good place to mount a defense.

The greatest fear, besides defending the Pass at Thermopylae, was that the Persian Army would come around and flank us from the sea. For this reason, we placed all our trust in the Athenian Navy. Their job was to protect our flank and keep us informed if that flank broke. Having had an up-and-down relationship with Athens, we were on new ground trusting them to defend our flank.

The Athenian admiral was also a politician. Themistocles and I knew each other, but not well. He, however, was confident in his skill and seamanship that he could mount an adequate defense and protect our flank. So, he led the Athenians as well as other allies who provided ships.

When we arrived at Thermopylae, we were to rendezvous with Themistocles. I was looking forward to this rendezvous.

Prior to getting to Thermopylae, the remaining allies joined up with us including the Thespians, Thebes, and troops from Phocis. This was a welcome addition to our troop numbers. Aside from late arriving individuals or small groups of soldiers, the coalition had now achieved its full strength as we reached Thermopylae.

CHAPTER FOUR

ARRIVAL

First Day at Thermopylae

*Kallidromo sings to welcome the Greeks as the sea
cools the summer air.*

There was a small village outside of Thermopylae. The village was called Alpeni. This village was a short walk from Thermopylae. It also had a small landing area for ships. This town mainly took its living from the water.

When we arrived at this town, we found it mostly deserted. It seems that many of the residents of this part of Greece had fled once they heard of the Persian advance. I decided that Alpeni would be a good area for all of our troops to camp.

I told my Captain Dien to have the Spartans set their camp in a location nearest the East Gate of the Pass. I said, "Once this is done, I want to meet with you and the other captains."

Dien nodded his understanding and the Spartans began setting up their camp.

I told Sari, "Set up my camp near the Spartans toward the East Gate." Sari went to work making our camp.

I walked to the East Gate of Thermopylae and found it to be very, very narrow. I stood and waited for my captains to join me. It took only a short time for this to occur. Dien was first to arrive followed by Kron, then Zee, Gelon, Illi, and finally, Dom. As Dom arrived, I jokingly told him it was good of him to join our meeting. Not acknowledging my humor, he nodded his understanding.

Illi asked, "Where is the gate?"

I explained to Illi that there are no actual gates. The areas at either end of the Pass, as well as the middle, are referred to as "Gates" due to the narrow passages. I looked around my semi-circle of captains pointing out that our meeting is almost taking up the entire twenty-foot width of this Gate.

I told the captains to follow me as I turned to begin our walk through the Pass. The most notable feature was our right flank which consisted of a cliff with a vertical drop-off measuring between 60 and 110 feet. The bottom of this cliff connected to the Malian Gulf. Just passed the East Gate, the area opened up to a wide expanse of land. Cart tracks marked the path most often taken through the Pass. This area widened from hundreds of feet to almost a mile in width.

I noted that very little of this part of the Pass would be suitable for our battle tactics. Although there is some open field, the area gradually sloped upward toward the Kallidromo Mountain. In some places, the slope becomes severe. The field is also not barren. There are numerous shrubs, small trees, and many disbursed rocks and boulders.

As our walk continues, I observe over my shoulder that my captains are assessing the area as well. We hike approximately two miles before arriving at the old Phocian Wall in ruin. I explained to the captains that this area is called the Middle Gate or the Hot Gate. The name, Hot Gate, references the nearby sulfur springs that come out of the mountain. In looking the wall over, it was evident that it would require much work for it to play any part in our defense of the Pass.

We walked through a narrow opening measuring fewer than fifteen feet to continue our observations. Just beyond the wall, the Pass narrows measuring between fifty and sixty feet wide. On the right, the vertical cliffs descend to the sea. The top of the cliffs is uneven making it impossible to walk a straight line along the edge. To our left, the mountain comes right to the edge of the Pass. The tall mountain is sheer and too steep to climb at this location. This area was free of large boulders. I was glad my captains were silently taking everything in.

As we continued, the Pass slowly widened after one hundred feet from the Middle Gate. This widening continued as the mountain to our left became less vertical, gradually sloping away. A mile from the Phocian Wall, the area began looking similar to the East-Gate-side of the Pass. The land widened out into a large field. This field gradually sloped upward making all but a half mile of width usable ground for battle. As on the east side, this area was also dotted with small trees and shrubs as well as rocks and boulders.

After walking two miles from the Middle Gate, we arrived at the narrow West Gate. This passage was approximately thirty-five feet across. Beyond the West Gate was a huge expanse of land where our enemy would most likely be camped.

I looked at my captains and said, "Remember what you have seen." We began our trek back to Alpeni.

I realized we would do this walk again with the leaders of the coalition, but by then, I would have formulated a plan for defending the Pass.

After returning to camp, I noticed the Spartans were relaxed and recovering from their journey and a short distance away, the perioikoi camp was doing the same.

I also noticed lines of supply wagons and food wagons that were setting up their camps, as well. We had brought extra food wagons along in anticipation of the rest of the Spartan Army joining us soon.

I thought, *At least, we will eat well while we are here.*

I realized that it would take the rest of this day and most of the next day for the entire force of coalition troops and their support to arrive and settle into the camp.

I told Dien and each of the captains, "Each of you will report the logistics of the Pass to your fifty men."

I also told them that I thought it would be wise to set up a guard at the East Gate and send some men to the edge of Alpeni and advise troops where to camp as they arrive. As each group arrives, have the leader report how many men they have brought. This will help me formulate my plan.

I dismissed my captains and went to my own camp. Sari had set things up nicely and it was getting to be late in the day.

I asked Sari to find Megis and also to bring a sacrifice to me.

Megis provided his reading. "Kallidromo sings to welcome the Greeks as the sea cools the summer air."

My mind was swirling with thoughts about how to best defend Thermopylae. I decided that I could not formulate such a plan until the rest of the coalition arrived and I knew exactly how many troops would be at my disposal.

Sari fed me a great meal. As I dined, I observed a small group of Spartans marching to the East Gate to take up guard duty.

I spent my first night at Thermopylae with many thoughts, but I did get good rest.

CHAPTER FIVE

GREEK SOIL

Second Day at Thermopylae

The Greek sails will shine brightly in the sun, their flags blowing from the wind of the Gods. The echoes of the mountain are hollow. The day will be peaceful.

W hen I awoke, Sari fed me and I told him, "Go get a sacrifice and bring the reader." Sari left with no further words. I could tell by the sounds that our camps had grown larger overnight.

When Sari returned with the reader, I took the small hen that Sari had brought, quickly killed it and handed it to Megis. Megis took his time with the reading and I waited. Megis turned to me and said, "The Greek sails will shine brightly in the sun, their flags blowing from the wind of the Gods. The echoes of the mountain are hollow. The day will be peaceful."

I looked at Megis and said, "I accept your reading." He nodded and left.

I told Sari to get my captains. This did not take long since our camps were adjacent to each other. I sat at my campfire as the captains arrived. I told them to sit with me.

I said, "By the end of the day, we will have to meet with all the leaders who are present. We cannot wait any longer. We will take them on a tour of the Pass and then I will advise them on how we will defend the Pass."

I asked my captains if they had any anything to impart to me prior to the meeting with the leaders.

Dom asked what I intended to do.

I looked at Dom and said, "I would rather wait until we meet with the leaders to give my opinions and orders on how we will accomplish our goal."

Dom nodded his understanding.

Zee spoke up asking, "Certainly, my King, you can, at least, divulge some of your plans to us?"

I looked at him and studied him for a moment. Zee had an honest face. Zee was also very direct.

I said, "Zee, you would not be questioning the orders of your king, would you?"

Zee looked to challenge me verbally and thought better of it and smiled and said, "No, Leonidas, whatever your decision is, you know we will follow your orders. We were just hoping for a little information."

I realized that this may very well be the most casual conversation that occurs while at Thermopylae.

I looked from face to face and said, "You are right. I have thought of an idea that I hope will make the coalition stronger; however, my idea could equally upset the coalition. So, my idea is this. I do not know the leaders all personally, but what I do know of them is that few of them are soldiers. This will be a battle for soldiers. I am going to ask each of you to lead your small Company of Spartans and embed yourselves within the various groups of the coalition. The coalition leaders may not like it, but I intend for you to command each group of coalition soldiers and set the example of how we intend to fight with the help of your small Company of Spartans."

This revelation brought smiles to my captains' faces.

Dien asked, "We get to lead the coalition troops?"

I looked at him and responded, "Dien, who better can lead this coalition other than Spartan officers?"

This comment brought nods and smiles all around.

I said, "For the time being, keep this information to yourselves and do not share it with your men. We will discuss this more later on. I want to meet with the leaders, who have arrived, late in the day at the East Gate. That should give us enough time to walk the entire Pass and return before dark." I dismissed my captains at this point.

Later in the day, my captains and I were waiting at the East Gate as the leaders of the coalition began arriving.

I began the meeting by asking the leaders who were present if they were all camped and settled in. I told them then, that with a small group of Spartans, we would go up to the Pass at Thermopylae and determine how we would defend it.

I asked Captain Zee to bring his Company of fifty Spartans to the Pass and set up a guard post at the Phocian Wall until the other leaders and I had assessed the area.

I told the Spartans who were going to the wall, "Armor up just in case."

My mind was racing now that we had achieved getting here. It had taken longer than I wanted it to take; in fact, it had taken much longer than it would have if it had just been the Spartans alone.

I asked the leaders to accompany me into the Pass without any further conversation. I said nothing during this tour nor did any of the leaders, but I noticed the other leaders studying the surrounding environment. After about two hours of looking things over, the leaders and I returned from the West Gate to the Phocian Wall.

The fifty Spartans had taken up guard duty at the Phocian Wall as instructed.

"The Phocian Wall or Middle Gate", I explained to the leaders, "is sometimes referred to as the *Hot Gate* in reference to the sulfur springs coming out of the mountain."

I told the leaders we would meet again at first light and I would present to them my strategy to defend the Pass.

Without any words spoken, they all agreed with gesture or nod. I released the leaders and my captains to return to their camps.

I turned to Zee and told him to withdraw his men to the East Gate but to maintain a guard through the night.

He set about doing this and I returned to my camp. When I arrived at my tent, I found my servant organizing my uniforms and armor.

I kept an area of the Pass in my mind and wanted to give it another look. As I started back to the Pass, a contingent of ten Spartans followed me.

I stopped and turned. One of my captains was leading them. It was Illi.

I looked at him and asked him, "Is this necessary?"

He said, "Yes."

I said, "Okay, but please keep a distance."

I walked back up to the Middle Gate at dusk. At this moment, I realized we own this Pass. This Pass is Greek soil, as is the soil beyond the Pass, and I had an overwhelming feeling that I had not had before.

It occurred to me, I was not defending Sparta; I was defending Greece. I wondered how many of the leaders with me felt the same way I did.

I studied the area again memorizing the terrain. Just beyond the west side of the Phocian Wall, both flanks would be very easy to defend, one flank dropping to the sea, and the other flank was sheer rock wall providing no path for the enemy to get around us.

Farther beyond the Phocian Wall, the mountains were still sheer at some points. As the field widened, the mountain became less steep and more hill-like. This worried me, and technically, it opened up our flank if we chose to fight farther into this field. I had some decisions to make and I had to make them all by myself.

I now perceived the men from all the different city-states in a new way. They were no longer just members from a specific place; they were all part of Greece.

I thought, *We are all Greeks.*

At that moment, I realized how selfish I was to just want to save Sparta without regard for what would happen to everyone else. I did not know how to convey these feelings to anyone else. So for the time being, I kept them to myself.

I returned to my camp through the East Gate with my Spartan escort.

I told Sari not to disturb me unless it was important and I went to my tent to rest.

I realized I must be very careful in dealing with the leaders of the various city-states. At the same time, I realized that I had to defend the Pass.

I lay down noticing the sounds of the various camps growing quiet. I reflected on the day; I would not be in this position had I not agreed to lead the coalition. But had I not agreed, who would have led the coalition; a politician, a carpenter, a stone mason? Who would have defended Greece?

I slept.

CHAPTER SIX

BATTLE PLAN

Third Day at Thermopylae

*The mountains sing Greek songs and the breeze from
the sea plays Greek flutes. The ground at
Thermopylae will remain calm today.*

S ari woke me at dawn advising me that the leaders and
my captains were waiting at my fire. I exited my tent
to meet with the other leaders including my captains
and told them how we were going to defend Thermopylae. I
explained that we had enough men to fight in shifts and that
no group would ever be on the battlefield without having
reinforcements and reserves ready to jump in if they needed
help. We would fight as a unit, as Greeks.

I told them we will perform using the phalanx and my
captains will provide information that will help their
phalanxes become better:

I know many of you are familiar with the phalanx, but you are not as knowledgeable of the Spartan phalanx. The information I now offer is to benefit those of you who are not regular soldiers. Our soldiers spend thirteen years practicing and perfecting the Spartan phalanx. The Spartan phalanx involves a group of soldiers forming rows of men where the front line soldiers form a straight line across and have subsequent lines directly behind them.

The phalanx begins as a defensive posture providing an impenetrable row of shields overlapping to the left. Each soldier carries a shield in his left hand and a seven-foot spear in his right hand. He also wears leg armor, chest armor, and armor protecting his forearms.

The large round shield covers the area from the knee extending up to the helmet protecting the neck. The round construction design allows the shields to overlap, providing greater protection along the front line of the phalanx. The shield is constructed using multi-layers of bronze and wood. What makes our shield unique is an adjustable fitted arm strap located near the center of the shield. The hand grip is nearer to the outer edge of the shield. The exact configurations of the parts that make up this grip are determined by custom fitting the shield to the soldier. The hand grip is made sometimes from wood, leather, rope, or some combination of these. This strap allows the soldier to have superior control of the shield. It is much more difficult for an enemy to knock the shield to one side or another because of this grip. I have instructed the perioikoi, who are along to repair our armor, to assist all coalition forces as time permits, by adding this feature to their shields. I particularly want this strap to be added to the shields of those who will be on the front two lines.

The helmet has narrow slits for breathing and eye holes. All soldiers are equipped with a short sword that is only used if their primary weapon is not available.

The Spartan Army is referred to as heavy infantry. This is due to the amount of armor each soldier wears or carries weighing as much as one-half their body weight.

Viewing the phalanx from the front, you would not detect an opening through the heavily armored Spartans. The Spartans are so confident of this defensive formation that they have no problem allowing an enemy to charge this formation in an attempt to penetrate it. Behind the first line, the subsequent lines of soldiers press their shields into the back of the soldier in front of them during the defensive formation. This provides an impenetrable wall that cannot be moved.

When it is decided to attack, the phalanx is ordered to disengage from the enemy that is pressing against them. This is done by stepping back in a coordinated maneuver. Once this occurs, the command is given for the front two lines to bring their spears up facing the enemy directing them toward the attacking force. The front line keeps their spears at waist level. The second line puts their spears over the right shoulder of the man in front of them using an overhand grip with the spears aiming downward. Upon command, the phalanx moves forward and thrusts both low and high. This coordinated attack becomes an organized killing machine. As long as the attacking force remains in the path of the Spartan spears, they will fall. The Spartans continue stepping forward and thrusting until the enemy breaks off, retreats, or is defeated.

There is also a triple-spear formation that utilizes our extra-long spears. During this maneuver, the third line switches their shield to their right arm. They use their left hand to hold their extra-long spears using an overhand grip while thrusting over the left shoulders of the first two lines of soldiers.

The phalanx can vary in size depending upon the tactical situation and number of soldiers available. So, as you may now understand, the Spartan phalanx is superior to any of your formations, even though, your attempts at the phalanx may outwardly bear some similarities.

Without divulging my personal feelings, I told them they need to look beyond their states and realize that if we are going to survive, we have to become unified. I added that some would have to fight right next to those who in the past had been enemies.

I did tell them, that for the time being, I would divide the Spartans and assign a small company to each fighting group. This way, Spartans will always be in battle. The leaders seemed to like this idea, and in fact, seemed to expect the Spartans to fight longer, harder, and more often than the rest.

Not one of the leaders tried to change what I was planning. They were basically leaving themselves in my hands and trusting me.

I further advised the leaders we would shore up the rock wall at the Middle Gate. I told them that if this wall was high enough, we could muster our troops behind it without being viewed by the enemy. "We would then put troops in front of the wall who would fight. By doing this, we would have fighting troops in front of the wall and reserve troops behind the wall.

"The next group of troops will be organized and mustered inside of the East Gate of the Pass, but a ways back from the Middle Gate. This should give us, at least, four regular groups to fight in rotation and maybe a fifth group to use as reserves."

The Thespian leader, Demophilus, asks, "How many men will we have in each fighting group?"

I looked at him and looked around at the other leaders and told them, "Hopefully, between twelve hundred and fourteen hundred men per fighting unit."

I further told them of my concern for the left flank. "If we have twelve hundred men, it will be a phalanx that will be at least one hundred men wide and twelve men deep. The reserves will have to watch closely and be ready to meet any challenge to our left flank."

The Thespian asks a follow-up question. "Why does the phalanx need to be that deep?"

I said to him, "Our troops will take up very little space on the battlefield compared to the enemy troops. They will have far more than twelve deep. They could have more than thirty or forty deep."

The Thespian asks, "Then how can we hold this position if they have three or more times the depth?"

I don't like where this conversation is going. It is starting to turn into a discussion of why are we here. I looked at each man in the eyes around the group, and I said this, "We can hold this Pass because we know how to fight using the phalanx, they do not. They are not organized to fight in this method."

The leaders nod.

At this point, I sensed I have a shaky group of people who are going to be very hard to hold together. I am afraid that at the slightest break of our position, they will all run and it will be me and my Spartans left alone on the field.

Before breaking up the meeting, I had one more piece of information to tell the leaders. The Spartans would be embedded in each group and a Spartan captain would command each group while in battle.

This information was received about the way I thought it would be received. I heard grumbling and observed side-to-side shaking heads and wondered if this was going to be the end of the coalition.

At this point, I stood and used my command voice and said to the leaders, "You chose me to lead you and that means you chose Sparta to lead you. Your chances of survival will largely depend upon the Spartan leadership that I will provide each group." I let this sink in a moment, and then I said, "You should be thanking me for allowing you to have Spartan leadership in each phalanx."

At this point, I added, "We need troops to rebuild the wall and make some areas on top of the wall flat enough to walk on and use as observation posts."

The Corinthian leader immediately volunteered his men as did the Phocian leader and the leader from Locris.

I told them, "We will meet again tomorrow and I will give you your phalanx assignments."

I dismissed the leaders from the meeting.

Captain Gelon asked for a brief conversation. We stood and faced each other. Gelon reported that troops and supplies were continuing to arrive. Troops had been still trickling into our campsite late throughout the previous night. Wagons were still arriving. We were camped over a spread-out area, so much so, that the troops at the back would probably have a half mile march to get up to where the front troops were camped.

I acknowledged this report from Gelon and thanked him and asked him to keep me informed.

I told Sari, "I will rest before breakfast" and went into my tent.

I realized that one of my biggest challenges was to unite this force into a productive fighting unit. I also knew that to be successful, there would need to be some changes in how the coalition viewed itself and each other.

I thought rest would be appropriate because I firmly believed that there would be very little rest in the coming days.

After a short while, Sari called me to breakfast.

I told Sari to go find the reader and bring a sacrifice while I dined. Sari left immediately.

I knew I had the support of my captains and the other Spartans, and quite possibly, some members of the coalition. Nonetheless, I felt very alone with the decisions that had to be made.

After a short time, Sari returned with a chicken and the reader. I thanked Sari and took the chicken.

Using my knife to kill and prepare the bird for the reader, I handed the bird to Megis and returned to my camp area.

After a short time, Megis approached me with a smile. "The reading for the day is all good for Greece. The mountains sing Greek songs and the breeze from the sea plays Greek flutes. The ground at Thermopylae will remain calm today." I thanked Megis and released him.

I spent much of the day in solitude; however, I did walk to the Middle Gate to find the wall being rebuilt by hundreds of troops. The wall was no longer going to be a major concern.

I found Captain Illi on the East Gate side of the Phocian Wall. He informed me that his troops were on guard duty in front of the Phocian Wall. I thanked him.

As I was walking away, he said, "All except for the ten who I have assigned to be your personal bodyguard."

I kept walking realizing that this was a fight I could not win. It occurred to me, *Maybe Illi's wisdom of guarding me is a precaution I should just accept.*

As I went back through the East Gate, I could hear the sounds of more wagons arriving which meant more troops were also arriving. I got to my camp and told Sari, "Advise each leader to keep me informed of the number of troops available for our defense."

I spent the rest of the afternoon and early evening making the decisions for my battle plan. I envisioned how the groups would fight and rotate in and out of battle.

The day ended without event. I went to my tent. Sari said, "Rest, King."

My night is sleepless. The pressure of trying to keep our defensive force together and out-think the sizable foe that is coming will not allow me to rest. At some time during the night, I had to have drifted off.

CHAPTER SEVEN

THE SPARTAN PHALANX

Fourth Day at Thermopylae

*The wind is rising. Dust from the West is in the air,
but the sun will shine brightly on Greece today.*

I was awakened in the morning by a noise outside my tent. My servant, Sari, entered the tent and advised me that my captains wished to counsel with me.

I told him, "I will be out soon." After getting dressed, I did go out where Sari was busy preparing a morning fire.

My six captains were present and waiting for my meeting with them. Dien began the meeting by advising me that they had seen signs that the Persians were arriving beyond the Pass and making camps. I took this information calmly.

I asked the question, "Is the wall construction complete?"

Dien responded advising me that there was a little more work to do on the wall and then it would be ready for use.

I told them that we would meet with the rest of the leaders later in the day to discuss our plans and tactics.

I then, as customary, told Sari to bring an animal for sacrifice and summon the reader. Sari immediately left.

While he was gone, I looked at my officers and told them, "I have grave concerns about the ability or desire of our allies to stand and fight with us." They made no comment to this statement.

After being a soldier so long and a leader of men, you get a sense of what people are feeling. It is a sense that goes beyond the mannerisms. It is a sense that is primal. It is hard to put into words, but you can feel the fear of a man.

My Captain Dom asked, "How will the Spartans disburse among the allies?"

I told him, "I have thought about this question much of the night. I would prefer that the Spartans fight as a unit, but given the tentative relationship with the allies, I still feel we will have to divide our force to accommodate their deficiencies."

I reminded my captains that there were very few soldiers here. Almost every other profession was represented, but not soldiers. Although our allies look like soldiers and dressed like soldiers and do have minimal skills; for the most part, many are not soldiers.

I looked around at my captains and said, "Keep this in your minds when you are dispersed amongst the allies. I leave it to Dien to divide our men in a way that every group that moves forward, will always have a faction of Spartans fighting within it."

Captain Zee asked, "What about the perioikoi?"

I responded:

The perioikoi are Spartan trained, but this will be a battle unlike anything they have experienced. We will embed with them, as well.

I stand by my order that we will field twelve hundred men in front of the wall as a fighting force. We have enough men to have three more rotations plus reserves.

So, you are probably asking; how can twelve hundred men fit into the small space beyond the Hot Gate? It is not wide enough to form a formation one hundred men across with twelve men deep, so the phalanx will be divided into two groups of men. The first-half of the phalanx with fifty men across and twelve deep will occupy the Pass. The second half will also consist of fifty men across, twelve deep and will be stationed slightly behind the first section of the phalanx. If the battle, or when the battle, moves beyond the Hot Gate area, we will need to use the second group of fifty to expand the left flank to cover the territory as the Pass becomes wider. This will permit our full phalanx to be utilized with one hundred men across, twelve deep.

As your king and general on this mission, I have viewed and considered what I feel may occur. If things happen the way I feel they will happen, we will not be able to stand our ground. We will have to advance for several reasons. One reason will be the buildup of bodies. A second reason will be to disarm archers and a third reason will be to allow more room for our troops to expand to a wider front and do more damage. This fight will occur between the Hot Gate and the West Gate of this Pass.

Accept these words, my Captains, for this is what I foresee. Go see to the wall now. Keep changing the guard beyond the wall. Make it known that the Spartans hold the Pass. Allow other troops to take their turn guarding. This will produce the effect of trust. Any questions my Captains?

"Just one question," asks Kron. "Where will you be during battle?"

I told my captains, "I will be at the front of the unit I choose to fight with. I will do my turn in a rotation as will all other soldiers. I cannot speak for where the leaders of our allies will fight, but I will fight up near the front. When I am not fighting, I will observe from the wall so I can make adjustments and give commands. Make sure, when the wall is complete, we have a way of getting on top for observation purposes."

I concluded this meeting. I told my captains to wait.

The reader arrived with Sari holding a chicken. I used a dagger to dispense with the chicken and opened it up. I handed the chicken to the reader.

After a pause, the reader smiled and said, "The wind is rising. Dust from the West is in the air, but the sun will shine brightly on Greece today."

I looked at my captains and told them, "Keep me advised." I dismissed them.

Sari asked me how I wished to dress for the day.

I told him, "No armor."

I proceeded to eat my meal that had been brought to me by the great helot cook that had accompanied me on other campaigns.

After I finished my meal, I noticed a commotion in the Spartan camp and was surprised to see a new group of Spartans who had arrived. I wondered if our Council had broken the law and sent the Spartans without the festival completed. I waited by my tent to see who had arrived.

The men who came to my tent and presented themselves to me in a loose formation were what would have to be described as *retired soldiers.* They had old armor, old shields, and were accompanied by a few helot servants.

A man approached acting as spokesman. He said, "We are no longer in the army, but have served our time. We are here as volunteers and Spartans."

I looked at this group and wondered if they could really help us. But, being in the position that I was in, I was not going to refuse any form of assistance. I welcomed the men and insisted that they set up their tents in an area close to mine.

These men had long since left the army and I questioned them, "Aren't you afraid that you have broken Spartan rule?"

One of the old ones spoke to me saying, "We are no longer in the army. The rules do not relate to civilians, and if they do, perhaps we can gain clemency from the King."

At this, I smiled.

I told Sari to find one of my captains and bring him to me.

The old ones were establishing their tent area with the help of the servants who had come along.

I stood and watched these men and wondered why they would do such a thing. I thought that this is the kind of thing I would probably do if I was in their shoes.

Sari appeared with Captain Gelon. I told Gelon to see that he found a space in our phalanxes for the men who had just arrived.

Gelon looked at me and asked, "Leonidas, are you sure these men can handle this work?"

One of the old men with sharp ears overheard us. He looked at Gelon with a scowl and said, "I can out-march you or outfight you any day young man." He followed up with, "I was in battle before you ever were allowed to be in the Agoge."

At this, Gelon remained silent.

I looked at Gelon and said, "Will there be anything else?"

Gelon gave a negative nod and left the area.

I looked over at the old man and smiled. I didn't want to leave it the way it was, so I said in a reasonable voice, "Thank you, Spartan."

As I left my tent area, from out of nowhere appeared my bodyguard of ten Spartans. I turned advising them, "Please give me space and stay a distance." There was no comment and they did stay back a bit.

I walked up to the Hot Gate and was pleased to see about five hundred men putting the finishing touches on the rebuilt wall.

It was also good to see, as I passed through the Gate, that on the other side were fifty Spartans standing in *ready position*.

I walked past the Spartans into the broader section of the Pass toward the West Gate with my bodyguard in tow.

In the distance, you could clearly see the activity of the enemy troops gathering. They were stirring up a lot of dust.

The Pass itself lends the winds a tunnel effect; therefore, if the wind is blowing toward us, then we have to feel their dust.

As I looked out into the Malian Gulf, I could see many Greek ships prepared to defend our right flank. I could not count ships from this distance, but it was nice to know that Themistocles and the naval forces were stationed to defend our position.

I returned to my tent area feeling that any rest I could get now would buy me strength later. I told Sari, "Allow me to rest unless it is important."

If you are in charge of something as big as this, and as many people are depending on you as this, the weight itself becomes an enemy. I pondered that I had no time to think of my family. I could not think of my wife or son except in a fleeting way. I now had to put my full attention and thought into defending this Pass to protect Greece.

I was a Spartan who was becoming *Greek*. I needed the others around me to also become Greeks.

We were not thinking, or let's say, I was not thinking about what would become of Greece one hundred years or one thousand years from now. I was thinking about Greece's survival today.

I did know that Greeks were unique. For the most part, we considered ourselves *free peoples*. Each city-state had its pluses and minuses.

I myself, a king of Sparta, had no trouble coming up with a list of deficiencies for our ways. Some city-states admired us and some just plain feared us. But, that doesn't mean that we were always right and that justice was always served. Sometimes, our traditions, laws, and rules, got in the way of what would be deemed just.

I rested. Rest did not last long. I was awakened by Sari telling me that the other allied leaders wished to meet with me.

I told him, "I will be out."

When I came out of my tent a few minutes later, I met up with all the leaders and officers of the various allied troops. In addition, my captains were in attendance. They wanted to know what my plans were and if anything, had changed. I sensed their nervousness.

It was now common knowledge in the camps that the Persians were gathering beyond the West Gate. I told them, "It is going to take a while for the Persians to get in position to attack if our scouts and spies are accurate."

I further advised them, "It has been reported that Xerxes has over a million men including foot soldiers and cavalry. Keep in mind that every country or city that he overran, he subjugated. His army is made up largely of slave labor. It is our understanding, as Spartans, if you do not fight for Xerxes, he will kill you. So, you see you are facing an enemy that fights to merely survive."

A leader from Thebes asks, "Isn't that what we are doing, fighting to survive?"

I looked at him and said, "Yes, but no one is holding a sword to your neck saying, 'You must fight.' Xerxes is fighting for domination. We are fighting for freedom. You must understand this, leaders, or you are at the wrong place or maybe on the wrong side." I looked down a moment wondering if I had gone too far.

I then looked up and said:

The orders of the day; there was a good omen passed for Greece today. We are in the sun. The orders will stand. We will fight in groups of twelve hundred. Since twelve hundred men cannot separate into one hundred across at the Middle Gate, we will be fifty across. If it becomes necessary to advance the phalanx into a more open area toward the West Gate, we will use the entire one-hundred-man front. This will prevent our phalanx from being flanked on the left. The cliff and the water will protect us on the right.

My Spartans will fight as a unit, but they will be embedded into our four groups of twelve hundred. We will lead. We just hope the allies will follow. The remaining Spartans will be available with another contingent, as reserves, behind the Gate.

If there are no questions, I have asked Dien to handle the organization of the various fighting groups. I ask you to each take turns in the broad area past the East Gate where each group of twelve hundred can have a short time to practice under the direction of my captains.

Although all of you understand the phalanx, we are masters of the phalanx. We will offer some information that will make your phalanx more successful and effective once in battle. Each group of twelve hundred will drill for at least one hour, starting today to help perfect their use of the phalanx.

Normally, when the phalanx is on the battlefield, we do not make the front two lines of soldiers remain in place during an entire battle. Our tactics include a procedure that allows these front two lines to retire to the back of the phalanx formation in a so-called *changing-of-the-guard* maneuver. As you can imagine, the hardest positions are where the battle is actually taking place engaging the front.

Due to the confined fighting area of this Pass and the fact that we are utilizing combined forces, we will not be able to rest the men on the front two lines. However, if a group has to fight a second time that day, those men will be placed in the back of the formation. Because of this issue, we will try to disengage from the enemy in a timely manner and will not unnecessarily prolong an encounter.

No questions were raised to me. I dismissed the leaders telling them, "Let's get to work."

At approximately noon time, I observed the first group marching past the East Gate for their practice with my captains. This first group included the perioikoi, fifty Spartans, and approximately four hundred men from one of the other city-states.

Dien assembled all available Spartans, who were not on guard duty, to put on a short demonstration of the use of the phalanx. I went through the gate and to the upper slopes of the field to observe this demonstration. Dien had a small phalanx of two hundred men in full battle gear assembled on the field. Beside me stood the perioikoi as well as the Greeks who would fight in their phalanx.

Dien began his demonstration by silently bringing the phalanx to *ready position*. In the ready position, the soldier stands with legs shoulder-width apart, helmet down, shield up, and spear by his side in a vertical position.

He then spent the next ten minutes showing the various capabilities and precision of the Spartan phalanx. He demonstrated *spears position, expanding the phalanx, advancing the phalanx,* and many other combat tactics. At the end of this demonstration, Dien addressed the crowd and said he would now demonstrate the method that would be used by the coalition forces. Captain Dien then demonstrated the *passing of orders* from commander to the men. He showed how one-word commands, passed from the left and right and to the lines behind, were able to elicit various maneuvers.

He then rejoined his phalanx with a loud verbal command, "Phalanx, READY." Quickly turning his head left, then right, he passed the *preparatory command,* "All" followed by the *command of execution,* "SPEARS." Upon his command of execution, the front two lines brought their spears up in unison facing the imagined enemy.

Observing from my location, you could see the soldiers on the front line, and each subsequent row of soldiers, passing the message from left to right creating a cascading wave of controlled movement as the command was passed from man-to-man.

At the conclusion, the maneuver was carried out in unison following the command of execution. This was done with such practiced precision that the onlookers offered loud cheers at the conclusion of the demonstration.

Although the perioikoi already possess the Spartan fighting tactics, it was important that they take the field to coordinate their efforts with the other men assigned to their phalanx. At this point, the other coalition soldiers had gathered on the slopes to watch the perioikoi practice.

Dien, along with the other captains, were working to make sure that the various phalanx groups understood all the basic commands and how the commands work to create the successful phalanx.

Dien had assigned himself to be the commander of the perioikoi phalanx. For this reason, he took the field with them allowing the other captains to assist in the instruction of the group.

The practice began with my captains standing in front of the seated phalanx so that they could observe what effect each command had.

Dien addressed the seated phalanx in a loud enough voice that the soldiers on the slopes could hear:

Aside from the formation itself, the commands directing the phalanx are what bring its effectiveness to life. The Spartans have had many years of training to perfect the various maneuvers of the phalanx. We can effectively perform all functions using voice commands, hand signals, or flute commands. Your phalanxes will operate by voice commands. An important fact to remember is that in most situations, the front two lines are the only soldiers who need to receive spear commands. It is the responsibility of the rest of the lines to always keep their eyes forward observing when these commands are given.

Commands that involve movement need to be passed to the entire phalanx. The preparatory command will be passed through the entire phalanx using one word. When the captain knows all have received it, the command of execution is given. The command of execution is not passed man-by-man through the phalanx. It is given as a one-word verbal command for the entire phalanx to hear. An example would be the preparatory command "Back" being passed through the phalanx. The phalanx is now prepared to step back once the captain gives the verbal command of execution "STEP." Once this is done, the group functioning as a unit will begin stepping back until other orders are given.

We have simplified the phalanx commands to accommodate the shortened training time we have available. We will instruct you on three basic types of commands. These will be *formation commands*, *movement commands*, and *spear commands*. Each type of command is essential for the successful functioning of the phalanx.

At this point, Dien took command of his phalanx while the other captains observed from a short distance away. Dien began by passing his preparatory command, "Phalanx" to his group. Once received, he gave the command of execution, "READY." Dien continued with the perioikoi phalanx practice.

As I watched this occur, I realized that there is a very large gap between our professional soldiers and the civilians who have come to help us. I was pleased to see the fifty Spartans embedded in the front-middle of the phalanx, ten across and five deep. It was explained that the coalition leaders would be placed in close proximity to the Spartan captain to assist in facilitating the passing-of-commands.

Once Dien felt comfortable working with his phalanx, he marched them forward to continue their practice a little farther inside the East Gate.

Meanwhile, the Thespians and Thebans took the field next to receive the same instruction. This was to be Zee's phalanx and also the phalanx that I decided to fight with. During the practice, there was much stepping on toes and running into each other. But after one hour of practice, this phalanx was also functioning adequately on a basic level.

Later practice included bringing out helots by the hundreds to holler and make noise simulating battle sounds. This gave each phalanx an idea of how limited verbal commands can be. During these sessions, the groups learned the absolute importance of paying attention to the front. The men came to understand that if you are not among the front two lines, you need to be ready to react when you observe what is happening in front of you.

The Thespians and the men from Thebes, along with their fifty Spartans, would be the first to take the field when it came time to defend the Pass.

Satisfied that the practice was going as planned, I spoke with Kron briefly.

I told him, "Get with the other captains and make sure that each phalanx knows how to defend against an arrow attack."

I left the practice area and went to the Hot Gate. The wall was finished and some of the Spartan guards were on top. I ascended a sturdy ladder that had been built acknowledging the Spartan guards when I arrived on top of the wall.

The wall was over twenty feet high and extended and connected with the mountain to the left and to the cliff to the right. There was an opening at the right side of the wall to allow access. There was no actual gate at this opening. The opening was approximately fifteen to eighteen feet wide.

From this vantage point, I could see well into the Pass in the direction of the West Gate.

I was pleased with my decision to fortify this wall and make our defense around the wall. The stone workers of several city-states had accommodated my wishes by fitting the rock and forming a crude mortar. The wall was now totally functional and the foundation of our defense. The top of the wall provided a walkway that was several feet wide.

I walked back toward the East Gate to watch Dien's phalanx practicing. As I watched the practice area, this group did very well being that the perioikoi already had basic Spartan training.

They went through the motions. They practiced the closed tight formation of the phalanx, each man shoulder-to-shoulder with the man next to him, shield in left hand, spear in the right hand, shields overlapping to the left, twelve lines deep, each man lined up behind the man in front of him with as little space as possible.

I was pleased to see that Dien was practicing passing up spears to the front two lines. The men on the front two lines would throw their spears down simulating the spear being broken during battle. This was followed by the soldier calling over his shoulder, "spear." The soldier would follow this command by reaching back to accept the spear from the man behind him. This was repeated throughout the lines. During battle, extra spears are brought to the soldiers in the back of the formation, as needed.

Dien not only is an exceptional officer but as I observed, an excellent teacher as well. I watched as Dien lectured, "The tighter the formation, the stronger the formation. Each man needs to view himself as part of a unit, not as an individual. If the unit moves forward, everyone moves forward; if the unit moves left, everyone moves left. A major role of the phalanx is to never allow the formation to be penetrated. If the phalanx works as it is supposed to work, it is an impenetrable wall that, after making contact with the enemy, begins killing the enemy using a methodical and practiced method." The drills were highly successful in preparing for the battles ahead.

The decision had been made to use verbal commands due to the complex nature of flute commands and hand signals. I agreed with my captains in making this decision.

I did intend to use flute commands from the wall because they would be able to be heard by the Spartans who would understand the commands.

As I watched this practice, I noticed other leaders, who had come onto the field, were observing as well. I felt this was important. It began to give me confidence that they would stand and not falter.

The Thespians did extremely well and had received our assistance in the past with their military training.

Other groups observed the practice, and when their turn came, they were prepared to do as instructed. By allowing the troops to observe, I learned it gave everyone more confidence.

The spirit of the group was changing. I could feel it. My captains could feel it, and I started seeing a new resolve in the leaders and the troops they were leading.

The day ended without event as far as conflict goes. However, at night, there were more fires visible past the West Gate than could be counted. This did, once again, create apprehension in our troops.

I went to bed realizing that no matter what I said, or what I did, part of what occurred here would be out of my hands. For, in the end, a person can only account for himself.

I did rest better that night.

CHAPTER EIGHT

MOUNTAIN PATH

Fifth Day at Thermopylae

The Greek sails now bear the lambda. Sparta and the Greeks are still under the sun, but a cloud is coming.

B y morning, Sari woke me asking that I come to the fire for a meeting. I told him that I would be out. When I arrived at the fire, one of my captains was present with several Spartans. The Spartans were holding a small man by the arms. I asked what was going on.

Illi said, "This man came to our forward position in the early hours. We did not kill him because he was not armed. He has a story to tell and he is Greek."

I looked at the man and asked him, "What do you have to tell?"

"The masses of Xerxes's men are building," he said.

I told him, "We know this."

He responded, "There is word in the Persian camp that they are trying to find a way around you."

I smiled at the man and said, "We are protected from the sea."

"I am not talking of the sea. I am talking about going through the mountains," he said as he shook his head.

I looked at him and stated, "There are stories of a way through the mountain. We do not know if a path exists."

"There is a way and Xerxes and his Persians are looking for it," the Greek replied.

I told the man, "Thank you and you are free to go." He left immediately.

I told Illi to get the other captains and bring them to my tent.

I instructed Sari to get the reader and bring the sacrifice.

I started thinking; I had ignored the idea of a path through the mountains because it had not been obvious.

After Sari brought the reader and the sacrifice, I asked him to summon the leader of the Phocians.

I killed the lamb and let the reader do his work. The reader told me, "The Greek sails now bear the lambda. Sparta and the Greeks are still under the sun, but a cloud is coming."

I thanked the reader and instructed him to give the lamb to the helots for cooking.

My captains arrived and I asked them what they felt about the Pass and the reported path behind it. They, like me, had considered it a rumor up to now.

I told them to wait as I had summoned the Phocian. I told my men that the very wall we had been rebuilding was originally built by the Phocians for a similar reason that we are using it now. I said, "The Phocians know this area. If anyone knows of a path through the mountains, it will be a Phocian."

While we waited, I asked my captains how they felt about the practice involving the phalanx. Collectively, they all seemed to be positive but were glad that there would be Spartans in each phalanx to help maintain order.

Zee made a comment. "The coalition troops have grasped the basics of the phalanx, but I wonder if their fighting spirit is up to the task at hand. Just because you know how to eat food does not mean you know how to catch it and kill it."

I looked at Zee and said, "Your concern is noted. Do you have any suggestions other than our current plan of embedding Spartans in each phalanx?"

Dien said, "Perhaps, the captains need to spend some time associating and interacting with these troops that we will command."

"I agree with you, but we have to be careful with the existing leadership of the coalition forces. Perhaps, you Captains would be best advised to spend more time with the coalition leaders and hopefully, enlist their aid in instilling the fighting spirit that is needed." Dien nods his agreement as did the other captains.

"In the event that I need you elsewhere, choose a second-in-command who is capable of taking over the phalanx in your absence. In addition, I do not want the Spartans to be exclusively on the front two lines of the phalanx. It is enough that we are participating in each phalanx. Also, when the other troops follow our directions and have success, they will gain confidence and be the better fighters for it."

At that moment, the Phocian leader arrived. I asked him directly, "Do you have knowledge of a path through the mountains that could be used by the Persians to come around behind us?"

He said, "No, but I will ask my men since there are people who have lived in this area." That was the end of the meeting. I told my captains to carry on.

I left for the Middle Gate. As I approached the wall, I noticed several Phocian guards standing on top of it and assumed that the Phocians were on duty at the time.

I climbed the wall and looked in the direction of the Persian camp. Beyond the West Gate, I could see colorful tents and clouds of dust and dots that had to be men and beasts off in the distance as far as I could see. I knew; once I had observed this, our meeting with the Persians would be coming soon.

I returned to my tent to find an emissary waiting who told me he was to act as a communicator with the navy. He said that the alliance's ships were in position and were ready for a defense of our flank.

I told him that I knew nothing of naval warfare or strategies and that I totally trusted the Athenian admiral, Themistocles, and the other naval leaders to do what they had to do to protect our land forces. We ended the meeting at that and he left rapidly.

Later that afternoon, the leader of the Phocians approached me with one of his soldiers. He advised me that this soldier knew of the path, but thought it was of no consequence because it was hard to find on our side of the mountain and was near impossible to find on the Persian side of the mountain.

He said, "The path is narrow and rough," and "that anyone traveling on it would have to walk in single file, especially, if they were carrying weapons and shields."

I asked the Phocian, "How long would it take a group of men to reach our location if they traversed the path?"

He estimated that it would take more than a day, maybe two.

I thanked them both and added that I would probably need the assistance of the Phocian to find the path.

I told Sari to find my captains.

I waited and thought. A good general does not leave a back door unattended.

Before my captains arrive, I have already decided that I must send some of our men to guard this path. This is disturbing because it will weaken our defense of the Pass. I have no choice.

The Phocian did not tell me exactly how long it would take to get here, but now I need to know how long it would take to get from the head of the Pass on our side down to Alpeni. This knowledge could be critical to the very survival of this defensive force.

My captains arrive. I look at them and explain what I have learned from the Phocian.

Dom questions, "Can we trust the Phocian?"

I looked him in the eye and said, "I don't know. Why don't you go find out? You go with the Phocian. View this place. Tell me how we can best defend it, and how long will we have if it comes under attack."

He asked, "When should I do this?"

I said, "Now, leave immediately. The Phocian leader will provide you the guide who knows the way. Report back as soon as possible." Dom leaves.

I look at the rest of my captains. I do not know what to say to them. We have made a plan which we have to stick to, but now we are going to have to spread ourselves thinner and commit some of our troops to this path.

Kron asks, "Should we send Spartans?"

I said, "No, we cannot spare any Spartans for this task."

Illi asks, "If Xerxes finds the path, how many men do you think he will send?"

I said, "He will send enough men to guarantee that they can surround us without us breaking through them to escape." No one spoke. I could see a bit of dejection on my captains' faces.

I told my men, "Muster the various phalanxes and continue your practice today. My belief is that tomorrow it will not be practice. As I look at you all, I hope I am in error."

I felt it was a good idea to ask my captains to keep training the various troops for several reasons. The first being, it gave them something to do with purpose and would hopefully, keep their minds off the Persians.

I retired to my tent. Sari stepped in and reminded me that I had not yet eaten.

I told him, "I need to rest."

I lay down and began to think. My position at Thermopylae is becoming more and more complex. I know that I, along with all the allies and my fellow Spartans, am getting ready to face the largest army ever assembled. For the first time, I realized that we are facing insurmountable odds. This army that faces us will stop at nothing to get through this Pass. I now wonder that if I had the entire Spartan Army present, would I be able to hold this Pass. I am very glad these thoughts are private and cannot be shared with my men; for if they heard them, they would certainly leave Thermopylae.

Before I came to Thermopylae, the oracle stated that a king must die.

When you fight alongside your men, that is always the risk, and that risk has faced me before. But, to think that all these men may die, as well, is a heavy, heavy burden to bear. Yet, they are all looking to me for confidence and leadership. If they knew what was in my head and understood warfare as I do, I doubt many would stay.

The Spartans are different. We were raised and taught how to be warriors from small children up through our adult life. It is a way of life to us. It is our honor. No Spartan will leave the battlefield. That, I can assure. It is our way. The Spartans embody what you would call *indomitable spirit*. This spirit does not permit the idea of defeat nor giving ground to the enemy. This spirit is molded into each Spartan soldier and is as much a way of life as breathing the air. The Spartans will stand. This is an absolute fact.

I must rest.

I was awoken by Sari telling me that I was being summoned to the Hot Gate.

I immediately left to go to the Hot Gate with my ever-present escort. Arriving thirty-five minutes later, I found the Thebes on guard duty. The captain of the Thebes said, "There is an emissary waiting beyond the wall to speak with you." He asked if he should escort me.

I said, "No." I looked behind me and told him, "I already have an escort."

I walked to the gate and found a mounted soldier wearing colorful clothing and holding a flag. I approached him and told my escort to stay back. I walked up to within twenty feet of him. I asked, "What do you want?"

He responded, "Are you Leonidas?"

I said, "I am Leonidas."

He stated, "I will deliver my message. Our great leader and god, Xerxes, wishes to offer you an opportunity to live. He states; if you will abandon the Pass, he will allow you to live. However, he will require for this gift that you fight on his behalf against the rest of Greece."

I looked at the emissary and said very slowly, "We will fight, but not *our* people, *your* people."

He asks, "Is this your final word?"

I looked at him, turned and walked away. I heard his horse turn and ride away at a gallop.

I went back toward the Gate. The guard that was assembled there, the Thebes, came to attention as I passed through.

As I went through the Gate, the Theban captain asked, "What happened?"

I looked at him and said, "He asked us if we wanted to surrender."

I could tell that he was waiting for an answer from me by his questioning eyes. I walked a few paces and hollered over my shoulder, "Hold your position, Captain, the Pass is ours and ours it will stay."

I walked on. On my way back to the camp, it occurred to me that perhaps our men were going to be staged too far from the battlefield. At this moment, it is my intention for all fighting to occur on the other side of the Phocian Wall. I decided I won't take any action at this time as far as moving our camps closer.

I arrived back at my tent with the intention of telling Sari to gather the leaders, but word of the emissary had preceded me. Already at my tent area were the leaders and officers and my captains, all waiting for my arrival.

Without waiting for a question, I advised them of the emissary's offer posing the question, "Would any of you like to go cross through the West Gate and go fight for Xerxes? That is what he is offering for you to do."

There was silence among the leaders.

I looked around at them and said, "Our plan stands."

The Thespian leader asks, "Any news of the path we have heard about?"

The leader from Corinth stated that he heard that the path would bring troops down behind us.

I told him as I looked around the group, "As we speak, we are scouting this path, and as soon as I receive the report from my captain, we will launch a plan to defend the path. I do not intend to allow this army to be flanked by sea or through the mountain. So, for now, concern yourselves with the Pass."

I paused and looked at them. I thought for a moment with my head down. They waited. I looked up. I said very slowly, "I trust you. We are allies. We are now about to face battle together. That makes us brothers. I will not lie to my brothers. I will not keep things from you. You must trust me as I trust you."

With this, there were nods from the group.

I said, "We will meet again soon." The leaders left, leaving behind me and my captains. After my captains had left, I was alone with my trusted servant who fed me heartily.

I then retired to my tent and my thoughts. I was wondering what information Dom would present when he returned from the path. I also wondered what was going on over in the Persian camp. Because of the wall, the Persians cannot get a good look at what is awaiting them. At this point, they just simply know we are holding the Pass.

As I rest in my tent, I can hear the work of the phalanx practice a short distance off. I know that days are very important now. When you are faced with such an adversary, with the amount of humanity that will be brought to bear on this situation, it is hard to fathom how anyone can stand up to this tyrant. Yet, here we are. The men I have with me are all I have. I cannot count on the rest of the Spartan Army to come and save the day. I am sure that very soon we will be tested here. I rest.

Early evening, I am awakened by Sari who informed me that Dom has returned with the Phocian. I go out of my tent immediately to receive his report.

Dom explains that the path is rough and narrow in many places after walking down it some ways. "It is defendable, however." He waits for my instructions.

I tell the Phocian that he can return to his unit and I thank him for his assistance.

I asked Dom to get the rest of the captains and bring them to me. After a short while, the captains arrive and I explained what Dom reported.

Illi asked, "How many men do you intend to send to cover the path?"

I responded, "I will send one thousand men."

"Who will you send?"

I answered. "We will send the Phocians. They are almost one thousand strong. That is about all the men we can spare from here."

Kron asks, "Why will you send so many?"

"Xerxes will not send a small force if he finds this path. He will send enough men to ensure that we cannot break out and retreat." My captains make no more comments.

I asked Sari to summon the allied leaders. While he was gone, I looked at my captains. I told them, "I have another plan."

I speak to Gelon, "I want you to ask the thirty retired Spartans if they are up to a mission. The mission would involve them going down the path, which I understand will be mostly a downhill trek for them. I want to know if they are willing to go into the Persian camp from the rear to try to assassinate Xerxes."

Gelon smiles at me and asks, "Do you think those old men are up to it?"

I looked at Gelon and explained, "I don't think it would be wise of you to bring up their age when asking if they are willing to do this. Their chances of success are probably all but zero; however, I feel it necessary to send some Spartans to attempt to kill the source of evil. This will probably be the last act these men perform for Sparta and Greece. So, I would ask them with great respect."

Gelon nods in acknowledgment.

As this conversation ended, the leaders arrived. I did not mince words. I explained to them the report I had received concerning the path.

I advise them, "I am choosing the Phocians to defend this path, mainly because they are more familiar with this area than the rest of you. If Xerxes's men come up this path, we will have only a matter of a few hours to respond. The reason I want one thousand men there, is because, as a good general, I know the enemy will send a large sized force if they come."

The Corinthian leader expresses that this will severely weaken our defenses here. He points out, "If you do this, we will only have three groups to rotate." I let this information be assimilated by everyone.

Then I told them:

No, we will still have four fighting groups. Each fighting group will have approximately eight hundred men. Also, we have been receiving small groups and stragglers coming into our camps daily ready to fight from outlying areas all over Greece. These troops are being trained as they arrive and have been assigned to work with the group of Spartans who will function as the reserves. This group now numbers one hundred Spartans plus almost four hundred additional troops.

These troops have been drilling and practicing as well. Their tactics are to enter through the Hot Gate when a need arises. These men are not to be taken lightly and have received extra training by my captains. These men will fight any time that there is a break or a need. So, we will have four groups of eight hundred each backed up by a group of five hundred reserves.

The Phocians will need to leave immediately and march to the path tonight. They will be accompanied by thirty Spartans on a special mission. I suggest that the Phocians leave now.

The Phocian leader nodded.

Before he left, I instructed him, "Let us know at the first sign if the enemy is approaching the path. At that time, we will send you reinforcements if possible. If not, we will send you instructions."

The Phocian leader nodded his understanding and was gone.

I looked at the rest of the leaders and said, "Now, you know you are protected on your left flank as well as the flank that includes the sea. My captains will give you the reorganization first thing in the morning for group disbursements." I dismissed the leaders and told my captains to stay.

I looked at my captains and said, "Re-organize the groups at first light and try to get a small amount of practice with each group. Work from a smaller facing. We will still be able to expand the flank to the left, but we want to make sure that the phalanx is deep enough to stop the assault. I leave it to you to work it out. Dismissed."

My captains leave and I look to Sari and tell him, "I will go to sleep now."

I slept a restless sleep wondering if this would be my last day, but I don't have time for thoughts such as these.

CHAPTER NINE

THE GREEK STORM

Sixth Day at Thermopylae

The sky over Thermopylae will be blue, but the water will turn red. The tide will bear the splinters of Persian markings.

J ust prior to dawn, Sari woke me and stated that Captain Gelon wished to counsel with me. I dressed and went out to meet with Gelon. I told Sari to get a sacrifice and bring the reader.

I greeted Gelon. Gelon advised me that the Spartan men, who I had spoken of, accepted the assignment and left with the Phocians last night. He said, "They were honored to do this."

Gelon then reported that he and the other captains had decided on a forty-man front with ten men deep. "Similar to the original plan, the eight-hundred-man phalanx will be divided into two groups. The first section will be forty across and ten deep. This group will occupy the Pass. The second group will also be forty men across and ten deep. The second section will be utilized if and when the phalanx moves forward forming an eighty-man across, ten-deep formation."

I acknowledged his report.

He further stated, "The units will begin practicing within the hour. The Corinthians are on guard duty now and have reported activity near the West Gate. They don't see any troops gathering there yet, but there is activity near the Gate." I thanked Gelon for his report and dismissed him.

Sari arrived with Megis and a chicken. The chicken was dispatched and I turned to the reader.

Megis responded, "The sky over Thermopylae will be blue, but the water will turn red. The tide will bear the splinters of Persian markings." I thanked the reader and pondered his words.

As I was wondering what type of cryptic message this could be, I received a dispatch from a runner off of a boat. The dispatch advised that our navy was engaging and were preparing to defend our flank.

I told the runner, "Keep us informed." He immediately left.

I sat near my tent eating the meal Sari had prepared and realized I have very little knowledge of naval warfare and tactics. And up until now, I had not considered the nightmare that Themistocles and the allied ships must be enduring to try to outsmart the large Persian Navy. I hoped the blood that was spoken of in the reading was not Greek blood.

I thanked Sari for my meal and told him to get my armor ready.

I then walked to the East Gate and observed the phalanx practice with the newly organized units. The practice was paying off and many maneuvers were now available to these troops. They were operating as units functioning in a highly disciplined manner.

I noticed Illi and Dom standing up on the rocks giving orders and shouting instructions.

I also noticed that the transition from forty across to eighty across had become very smooth. Upon a command, the back group would do a left turn in unison, march to the left of the first group, stop, turn to the right, march forward and meet up forming an eighty-man phalanx, ten deep. It was a magnificent looking maneuver.

After I viewed this for a short time, I walked to the Hot Gate and climbed the wall. I could see activity at the West Gate; but as had been reported, there were no troops massing there.

I looked to the left of me and walked over to a soldier on guard and asked his name. He seemed shocked that I was speaking to him.

He looked at me and said, "My name is Samos."

I looked at Samos and asked, "Are you prepared to defend Greece?"

"Yes, King," he responded.

I looked at him and could sense his conviction. I nodded and left him.

When I got back down the ladder, several of the allied leaders had come up, like me, to look over the situation.

I looked at them and decided that the allied leaders should meet with me. I thought that a meeting at the Hot Gate would be a good idea. I expressed this to the men present and asked for a runner to go summon the rest of the leaders.

While we were waiting, we watched the phalanx practice. It looked good. The phalanx was facing us and they were now practicing the movement that does the killing; spears thrusting under the shield as the second line thrusts over and downward. This was done in unison and then they would take a step forward and continue.

After all this training, I hoped that our Greece would be united, so that these tactics we had so willingly taught are not used against us.

When the rest of the leaders arrived, there seemed to be an upbeat feeling among them. I felt that having several days here had provided the opportunity for us to solidify a plan to defend the Pass. This work had helped to bring the members of the coalition together. Even though we had to send troops to guard the mountain pass to prevent our position from being flanked, things still seemed generally upbeat.

I addressed the leaders by suggesting that we move some support functions up behind the wall to include aid for injured soldiers plus additional spears and shields. I also thought that it was important to bring a couple of the food wagons and water supplies close-by so they would be ready to refresh troops as they come off the battlefield.

I felt that we had done everything we could in preparation to defend this Pass.

I advised the leaders of the mission involving the thirty Spartans. I did not expect to have any result from that mission for at least a day. I felt like it was a tactic that would possibly have a good outcome.

"The Spartans are smart warriors. When they get to the back end of the path, they will come out a distance from the Persian camp. However, the Persian camp will not have guards posted in the area where the Spartans will arrive from. As I said, the Spartans are smart. They will wait till darkness to try to find and kill Xerxes. If they are successful, we will certainly know. I wanted to share this with you so you know that we have done everything we can in our defense of Thermopylae."

I further advised them of the report of the naval engagement. I told them that I would keep them informed.

"If we can get through without incident until late in the day, then I think we can assume that Xerxes will try to challenge us for the Pass tomorrow." I thanked the leaders for cooperating with my captains on the reorganization and disbursement of troops. I then left the group and headed for my tent.

I told Sari that I would wear my armor beginning tomorrow morning.

He advised me that it would be ready.

Later in the day, I walked down into the camps wanting to be among the soldiers who would soon be going into battle. I wanted them to become comfortable and realize that I was one of them, and I would be fighting alongside them.

As I walked through the various camps, the men were busy; some resting, some preparing their equipment, and some sitting around their fires and eating. As I approached each group of men, once I was recognized, they would stand. I immediately motioned them down. I was generally met with friendliness, and I did sense that there was a good feeling among the men for me having visited even though I was merely walking through.

What I was looking for were the food wagons. I love my servant, Sari, but sometimes you just want something different to eat. I realized this may be my last opportunity to enjoy something I wish to eat.

There were dozens and dozens of food wagons, some operated by helots and some operated by perioikoi. Also, some city-states provided food support and supplies in addition to their troops.

This was an interesting experience to walk among people who were concerned with keeping this massive army fed. Once again, as I walked among these people and was recognized, they would stop what they were doing and offer a slight bow. I nodded in appreciation for this.

I finally found what I was looking for, a wagon whose owner had brought bread. As I looked around, there was no one at this wagon at the moment. Feeling a little bit like a thief, I grabbed a small loaf of bread and started back toward my tent. Along the way, I began eating the bread and enjoying it.

As I walked along, I knew that nothing would ever be the same again in this camp, probably beginning tomorrow.

I returned to my tent with only half a loaf of bread remaining. I offered the other half to my trusted servant, Sari. Sari thanked me and I rested.

About midday, a runner came with information concerning the sea battles. He advised that the Athenians, along with the few Spartan ships and ships from other city-states, had fared well during battle. Many Persian ships had been sunk and some had actually been captured. The message did not go into details of the encounter but did express that Greece won the day.

I wondered if the reason Xerxes had not attacked the Pass was because he wanted to try to get around behind us with his ships. Each ship can carry a group of soldiers in addition to the oarsmen and the crew of the ship. I thanked the runner and he left immediately.

I was not being given enough information to take any more action than I had taken.

As I was sitting outside my tent, I watched as the last group of the day began their practice with the phalanx.

I thought, *If we could only have brought ourselves together as a country sooner, maybe we could have had better representation for such an event as this.* But, you know it is hard to judge the past.

Late in the day, I received word to come to the Hot Gate. I did so with my ever-present bodyguards accompanying me. Once I arrived, I noticed the Spartans were on the wall and in front of the Hot Gate.

Dom was present and advised me that another emissary from the Persian camp was waiting out front. I went immediately.

When I entered the area in front of the gate, there was a man about fifty feet away parked with a chariot and a flag. I also observed enemy troops well in the distance.

I considered for a moment that this might be a ploy to get me into the open for an assassination attempt. I realized that the only enemy close enough to do me harm was the emissary. I stayed back at the front of the guards and hollered to the man in the chariot.

He said, "I am here to talk to Leonidas."

I loudly announced, "I am Leonidas."

He said, "I have a message for you." He asked if I would come and get it.

I hollered back, "If you have a message, then deliver it. If it is in writing, you may deliver it. If it is verbal, you may deliver it; but, I stand among my Spartans." I waited.

The man paused; and then, he threw a tablet apparently containing a message down on the ground and rode his chariot back to the West Gate.

One of my bodyguards quickly ran and recovered the tablet and hurriedly brought it to me. I took the tablet from him and went back through the Hot Gate with my escort.

The tablet once again offered what the first emissary had offered. It was an offer to live with the stipulation that I and my men would fight for Xerxes. I handed the message to Dom and told him to keep it safe.

I knew that tomorrow Thermopylae would become a battlefield.

I told Dom to accompany me back to my tent.

Once we arrived there, I asked Sari to get the rest of the captains. Within minutes, the captains arrived. I told them that tomorrow the men should dress in their armor and prepare for war.

I asked, "Which group will be the first to defend the Pass?"

Zee said that he had been working with the Thespians and felt they would do a good job in the defense of the Pass. His fifty Spartans would be embedded with them along with some men from Thebes.

I asked if anyone disagreed with this. No one offered a disagreement.

I advised my captains of the report from the sea battle. They all seemed pleased.

It was getting to be later in the day and it appeared that a storm was brewing. I advised the captains to meet with each of the leaders telling them their positions and telling them to prepare for a storm this evening.

I told Illi, "For the time being, you are going to command the reserves and take over guarding the Hot Gate. Also, the rest of the reserves should be moved up to camp behind the Phocian Wall. Move up the supply wagons, medical wagons, and some of the food and water wagons." These orders were all spoken without any comment from my captains.

I asked if there had been any report from the Phocians. There was no word so far.

I excused my men and told them to return to their units and to pass on the information to the allies. My final word was, "Be ready to fight at dawn."

I felt no need to summon the other leaders when they were merely going to receive the information that I passed to my captains. The storm did come up that night, ferocious at times, but our tent held. As I lay there listening to the wind and rain, I realized that I could be no more than I am, and I could do no more than I have done. I didn't know if either of these things was going to be enough for the task at hand. I knew that tomorrow's battle would be unlike anything any of us had experienced.

Once again, it is hard to sleep when so much weight is on you. I have truly become a Greek as much as I am a Spartan. I hope that this will be realized even if it is not me that gets to tell it. Tomorrow, Xerxes will face a different kind of storm. He will face the Greeks.

CHAPTER TEN

HEAVY INFANTRY

Seventh Day at Thermopylae

The wind will blow out of the East. The Persians will feel the breath of Hercules in their faces. Greece will smile today. The sword will be red.

Before dawn, I am awakened by Sari. He tells me that all the leaders and my captains are outside waiting for counsel. I tell Sari to advise them that I will be out shortly and to summon the reader and a sacrifice.

I go outside my tent and find all of the leaders of the allied troops standing as well as my captains. All are wearing their armor but are not with their head gear, spears, or shields.

I smile and greet them, "Good morning, Greeks. Today will be different than any other day. You men and the men you have brought with you are my brothers. We will defend Thermopylae, and in doing so, we will defend Greece. Do any of you have any questions or not understand anything concerning your assignments?" I wait. There is silence.

I then told the coalition leaders, "None of us are near our homes and right now, all we have is each other. We cannot count on anyone but each other." I asked the leaders to wait.

The storm had blown over, but there was a cool breeze.

I turned to find Sari and the reader waiting. I went to them and dispatched a lamb. I turned to the reader and waited.

Megis examined the lamb. Then, he turned to me noting that all the leaders and my captains were standing patiently waiting.

He looked at me and said, "The wind will blow out of the East. The Persians will feel the breath of Hercules in their faces. Greece will smile today. The sword will be red."

I looked at the captains and the leaders and said, "Prepare your men. Make sure that each man is fed sufficiently. This may be the only meal that he gets until this day is gone." I dismissed the leaders.

I looked at my captains and asked them if they had any questions or concerns. I received no answer.

I told Zee, "I will fight with your phalanx and the Thespians. Once it is determined that the Persians plan to attack, we will take the field in front of the Hot Gate. Remember, they may attempt an arrow attack before committing troops.

"Illi, you will be in command of the reserves. Do not commit all of your reserves at once. If they are needed, send them out in companies of no more than one hundred.

"Dien, Kron, and Gelon will all take command of their phalanxes and embed in the next three groups.

"Dom will assist the reserves from the wall and will act as Illi's reserve. Is everyone clear?"

Everyone nodded, yes.

"You, Captains, will lead from the second line. I cannot afford to lose any captains. I will see you on the battlefield."

As my captains left, I realized that they had an important task ahead. A battle is like a puzzle. A captain must think quickly and make instant decisions.

I went back to my tent where Sari assisted me with my armor. I told him to make it a quick breakfast, and that I wanted to get to the wall.

After my breakfast, I walked with my servant to the front near the wall. When I arrived, the reserves were seated with their backs to the wall and resting.

Also present were the helot servants carrying the helmets, shields, and spears of the individual Spartan soldiers they attended to. This custom evolved due to the weight of the equipment. We do instruct our soldiers not to wear their helmets and carry their shields unnecessarily.

The helots will further assist each of their own Spartans between battles with first-aid, food, water, or anything else that is necessary.

Off to the left were numerous wagons to provide food, water, backup weapons, and shields. In addition, the first phalanx was resting and prepared to move through the Gate when necessary.

The next three phalanxes were gathering back behind the first phalanx and would come forward when called. It was decided, once the first group takes the field, the next group will move up behind the reserves.

The entry through the Gate is not terribly narrow so that a number of troops can rapidly deploy beyond the Gate. One maneuver that was not practiced was bringing a new group onto the field to replace a group that exists on the field. This was discussed but not practiced. It was felt at the time that it was more important to practice our phalanx tactics than to practice changing to a new phalanx. I just hoped that this would go smoothly when the time came.

The camp of the enemy was stirring also. It was impossible to see what was going on, but there was definitely activity in the distance beyond the narrow West Gate.

I looked around me at this mass of humanity wondering, *How did we get so many people willing to do this, risk death in such large numbers?*

As I stood and thought, I was approached by a runner. He delivered a message from our naval forces. The message stated that the night had gone well for our navy, and many enemy ships had been lost during the storm in an attempt to go around and outflank us. Our own ships had weathered the storm in some coves and made it through the storm without any losses.

I thanked the messenger and told him to report that the land battle was about to begin. He left immediately.

From the West Gate, I could hear loud trumpets blowing.

I was able to observe a device being pulled toward our position. As it got closer, it was evident that it was being drawn by oxen. It was placed less than a mile from our position. It was brightly colored and apparently was an observation platform for King Xerxes. I concluded that Xerxes wanted to have a good view of the battlefield.

I thought, *Xerxes is probably very frustrated if his navy has suffered losses on two separate days.*

I went up on the wall to get a better look and could see colorfully dressed soldiers marshaling about one mile away from our position. I could also see that Xerxes had stationed men as observers on the rocky cliffs about three-quarters of a mile away. I passed the word down telling Zee to prepare his men to take the field. The word was passed. Zee's phalanx formed up.

I told him I would replace one Spartan in the center of the second line where I would be stationed. This Spartan was told to hold this position until I joined the phalanx.

At that moment, a horseman came riding forward and rode to within fifty feet of the Hot Gate. The horseman shouted for Leonidas.

I was on the wall at the time and I shouted back, "I am Leonidas." I further hollered, "State your message!"

He said, "The great king and god, Xerxes, presents you his final offer. Leave the Pass and you shall live." He waited for my response.

I paused and I looked behind me feeling the breeze on my face. The only movement I detected was from the horsehair on the helmet crests and the Spartan war cloaks. I looked back at the rider and said, "The Pass is ours!" The rider immediately turned and rode off.

I told Illi, "Bring your guard from in front of the wall."

The fifty Spartans on guard, in front of the Hot Gate, came to attention, took one step back, performed an about-face maneuver and proceeded to march through the gate.

Once they had gotten behind the wall, I told Zee to bring up his phalanx. This was done and looked very good. As they approached the Gate, they stopped, allowing ten men and twenty deep to go through the gate at a time. They went to the field, and the first section of the phalanx formed up at approximately one hundred feet in front of the wall with the second section slightly behind the first. It only took a few minutes for all eight hundred men to get into position.

They went to rest position on one knee with their helmets pushed back and their shields on the ground in front of them. I noticed Illi had sent out a group of helots carrying extra spears. Some of these men stationed themselves behind the first section of the phalanx while the rest stood back against the wall.

We all waited. I observed that the group I had chosen to be a part of was ready.

I looked at Dom and said, "If something happens to me, Dien is in charge."

Before going down off the wall, I noticed twelve helot flute players were in position if Dom needed to send down an order to the Spartans.

The flute players always travel with the army to provide us communication on the battlefield:

As part of our army, helot flute players accompanied us on all campaigns. These flute players had multiple tasks in supporting our army.

When marching into battle, our normal gate was emphasized by accompanying flute music. We felt this did two things. It provided calming rhythmic notes to march to and intimidated our enemies. An enemy who observes us calmly walking toward them to flute music was sometimes unnerved.

The flute players also used their flute notes to issue commands by an officer during battle. When synchronized, twenty or thirty flutes can be heard above the roar of battle.

A third use is as entertainment both before and after battles.

I climbed back down off the wall. Before I left the Hot Gate, Sari handed me my helmet, shield, and spear.

As I walked by Illi, I told him to have his reserves ready.

I exited through the Gate and walked through the troops to the space that was saved for me in the second line. As I passed by the troops, they all stood. I dismissed the soldier that was holding my place, and he left immediately without comment.

I looked up and down the line. The fifty Spartans were embedded, ten across and five deep, in approximately the center of the formation. Zee was next to me.

I left the formation momentarily and walked in front of the troops and faced them. I spoke so all could hear me. I said, "Today you have the honor of being the first land troops to defend Greece. You will win the battle!"

At that moment, all the troops came to attention and put their spears forward in a salute. I nodded, in acknowledgment, and then I said, "Phalanx, RECOVER," which they did.

I made one final announcement. "Prepare for the initial assault to be made with arrows; follow the plans and tactics you have been taught and we will get through this without incident." At that, I walked back to my place in the formation, turned, and waited.

Zee asked me if it was wise for me to be wearing my cross-haired helmet.

I looked at him and said, "This is always the helmet I wear in battle."

Zee said, "Yes, of course."

While we waited, the dots of men in the distance became closer as did the platform that we assumed Xerxes would watch the battle from. Once they got to approximately one-half of a mile away, the platform stopped moving. It was surrounded with colorful flags and material.

The troops, who had come onto the battlefield, had extended the entire width of the field with line after line of men slowly marching forward. I was sure they thought that we would march out to meet them, but this was not our strategy. We stood and waited.

It was still fairly early in the morning, and the sun had not yet started heating the day. There was a cool breeze that refreshed us and made our wait not that uncomfortable.

The sound of the trumpets alerted us that the enemy troops were marshaling to engage us.

As we stood silently, I passed the order, "Phalanx, READY." Upon issuing this command, the men put their helmets down with their shields up.

I passed the preparatory command left and right, "Archers." The message was passed man-to-man, left to right, front to back with practiced precision.

There must have been as many as twelve hundred to fifteen hundred archers. It was hard from our vantage point to determine this.

Dom had the word passed down with a flute call to prepare for archers; not realizing, I had already given the preparatory command to prepare for archers. In addition, a flute call recalled all the helots back behind the safety of the wall.

The archers continued marching forward. I whispered to Zee that they were too far away to have any effect on us.

As the enemy continued to approach, we stood in our loose phalanx with approximately two feet behind each line. The enemy continued to move forward closing in on us. At approximately three hundred feet, the enemy gave their signals to fire their first line of arrows.

The arrows went into the air at a very high arch. Once they achieved their maximum height, I finished executing the archer order with the command, "DOWN." This was a loud verbal command that everyone heard.

The entire eight-hundred-man phalanx dropped to one knee and angled their shields at approximately a forty-five-degree angle covering themselves. We could hear the arrows in the air coming toward us.

As we heard this, we heard their captain's orders for the next line to "FIRE" as the first arrows hit. The arrows bounced off our shields partly due to the angle and partly due to the structure of our shields. We held our position as the arrows continued to rain down on us.

After the first few volleys of arrows, we were actually getting used to the fact that they could not penetrate our large shields. I was glad that the other city-states had adopted the idea of using metal in the construction of their shields modeling after the Spartan shields.

The rain of arrows continued through all the lines of archers and repeated with each line having several shots. Finally, their captain realized their distance was too great to achieve any success. At this point, he ordered their archers to march forward about one hundred feet.

As he did this, I gave the command, "Phalanx, RECOVER," and the phalanx once again stood up.

I believe that the Thespians, in particular, were amazed that they were able to sustain so many arrows without taking any injuries.

The archers were now one hundred feet closer. This would make little difference. I gave the command, "Archers" as the archers prepared to fire again.

As the archers released their arrows, I once again gave the command, "DOWN."

As the arrows hit, the result was pretty much the same. There were a few lucky shots that grazed some arms and caused some minor injuries. Also, some of the arrows flew over the wall, and I was able to detect defensive orders on the other side of the wall.

One line after another fired their arrows with little success. This went on for several more volleys from each archer. Once the captain realized this was not working, he ordered his troops forward another fifty feet.

I ordered, "Phalanx, RECOVER." While the enemy was still coming forward, I immediately ordered the Spartans to perform a special tactic. As the Persians were readying, I instructed the fifty embedded Spartans to remove themselves from the phalanx and extend beyond the phalanx into a single line, fifty men across.

I then ordered a running charge. This was accomplished in a matter of seconds. As this occurred, the archers became disoriented and confused by our actions. This was the last thing they probably expected. When we began our charge, their captain had his back to us.

As we approached the Persian archers, we closed our ranks remaining in a single line, and I ordered, "Low SPEARS." We stopped running and went to a slow but methodical march forward. We were advancing toward the Persians, shoulder-to-shoulder.

The Persian captain became aware of our charge when we were almost upon them. He ordered his frontline archers to fire at us. When this occurred, I ordered a defensive move that had us drop to one knee and angle our shields to the forty-five-degree angle. We did this with practiced ease. This maneuver allowed no arrows to penetrate our shields primarily because of the angle of our shields.

Upon receiving the first volley, I reordered the recovery to the line and continued the charge at a rapid walking pace. Upon seeing this, and realizing that their arrows had no effect even at this close range, the archers panicked and began to run.

As the archers turned to run, they ran into the next line knocking people over and creating complete panic in the Persian lines. The effect of this continued through each line of the Persians. They were now leaderless and in total disarray.

As we arrived at the junction of the first two lines, archers were trying to scramble to their feet to escape. Our spear-thrusts stopped a couple hundred of them from escaping.

I halted the charge and ordered the withdrawal at a rapid pace. The Spartans arrived back at the phalanx and re-took up their positions. I passed the word left and right, "Phalanx, REST." I looked left and I looked right, down the lines, and observed helmets propped back and a look on the faces of the Thespians that could only be described as *awe*.

I noticed, as the Persian retreat continued, the battlefield once again became calm. The only problem from the encounter was the thousands of arrows lying about on the ground amongst our phalanx. I viewed these as potential hazards.

At this moment, I could hear loud cheering. Apparently, Illi had brought a portion of the reserves out in front of the wall. Behind them were forty to fifty helots carrying water and extra spears. This group was cheering loudly. Among the cheers, I could hear the words *Sparta, Spartans, Lacedaemon,* as well as my name. I then went and stood in front of my phalanx. I held my spear up and hollered, "*Greece,*" as I struck my shield. My phalanx joined in. The men at the wall joined our cheer for Greece. Soon, the unifying cheers for *Greece,* followed by striking the spears against the shields, were echoing off the mountain. After several cheers, I returned to the phalanx.

Cheering during battle was not the Spartan way, but anything that made this group stronger and more cohesive was not to be discouraged. Long after we stopped cheering, we could hear the cascading effect from our troops behind the wall. It seemed to me that this release of emotion had a positive effect on our entire army of about 4000 men.

At this moment, Xerxes would have had to know, we are not going to abandon the Pass.

We stopped our chant as flute notes alerted us that new troops were forming up. Although the troops were still a good distance away, we could observe that there was a large mass of humanity forming in front of us. At that moment, I felt good about our position.

The troops who organized in front of us became too numerous to count. We calmly watched as they achieved their ranks. Then, upon orders of their captain, they began marching forward. They formed lines of men, end-to-end, covering the open terrain. Each line was spaced five or six feet apart.

The men we were facing were dressed in colorful clothing and had some sort of helmet that appeared to be made from leather. They were carrying spears and small shields that appeared to be made from wicker wood.

I noted that they had poor tactics. They were beginning their advance on us in a wider portion of the Pass but did not take into account that we were not going to march out and meet them. As they approached our end of the Pass, they were forced to bunch up and lose their positions of order. By the time they got to us, they would be highly disorganized. At least, this is what I thought.

I issued the command, "Phalanx, READY." I then issued the command, "Phalanx, CLOSE." The phalanx then became a compressed fighting unit.

Upon issuing this command, I felt the shield on my back from the man behind me. We were now an impenetrable wall of armor. We waited.

As I suspected, as the Pass narrowed, the Persian troops bunched up and were running into each other, stumbling, and in no way organized.

When they closed within approximately ten feet from our position, I ordered, "Phalanx, HOLD."

At this point, the front group of the enemy ran forward to engage us. As they did, their spears were parried either down or up without impacting the phalanx. As more of the enemy arrived, it became a bunched up mass of humanity. The phalanx held; no one moved as our wall of shields separated us from the enemy attack.

I gave the order, "High SPEARS." Upon this order, the second line put their spears up over the shoulders of the men in the front line.

I gave the command, "Phalanx, ATTACK." Upon this command, forty spears proceeded into the flesh at a downward angle of the men bunched against our front shields. These men fell.

As others stumbled into them, I repeated the order, "ATTACK." These men were penetrated by our spears in the same manner as the first group.

I now ordered, "All, SPEARS." As this order was received, the front line brought their spears up as well.

I ordered the phalanx forward to continue the attack. As we did this, the lower spears from the front line and the high spears from the second line thrust forward killing and maiming anyone in their path. The screams of the enemy and the blood of the enemy were everywhere. The enemy lines were so disorganized and now frightened at what was happening in front of them that they tried to turn, pushing against their own mass of fellow Persians.

As our attack continued, we were stepping over bodies. Some of these bodies were not dead until the third or fourth row got to them. These bodies were killed by the sharp spear-butts as we passed over them.

We were now a moving killing machine with men trapping other men in our path. We maintained the discipline of our phalanx and walked slowly forward. During this action, several spears were broken, but new spears were immediately passed up.

As we moved forward, the Pass began to widen. After it widened sufficiently, I halted the phalanx and ordered the second half of the phalanx to move up to our left. As this occurred, the phalanx advanced with both high spears and low spears forward killing many enemy soldiers who were trying to flank our left. Once the second half joined up, the new phalanx was now eighty across and ten deep.

Once again, I ordered the phalanx to move forward slowly and the killing and slaughter continued. We were losing many more spears than I thought we would.

Upon our continued advance, the enemy was in full retreat. I ordered, "Phalanx, HALT."

I then ordered a rapid withdrawal to our original position. At this time, I ordered the original right flank of the phalanx to take up the rear position and the left flank of the phalanx to take up the front position.

The enemy was in disarray and in retreat, at least, those that we did not kill.

I ordered the group, "Phalanx, REST."

Once I observed that the Persians were totally leaving the field, I ordered the phalanx to withdraw through the Hot Gate. The entire battle was over in about fifteen minutes.

From the wall, Dom saw what I was doing and hollered to Dien to prepare to advance.

My phalanx marched through the Hot Gate with smiles of pride that we had done what we came to Thermopylae to do. All the soldiers there knew that we could hold Thermopylae.

As the formation passed through the gate, I left the phalanx in the hands of Zee. Zee marched the formation to the rear for rest and recovery. As the phalanx marched to the rear, the rest of the phalanxes behind the wall honored them with cheering. This became a ritual showing respect to each group as they came off the battlefield.

I asked Illi to take a hundred men and a hundred helots and clear our end of the battlefield of dead and wounded.

He advised me he would do this and sent runners to summon the helots needed to do the task. He turned to me and asked, "What should we do with the bodies?"

I pointed to the cliff. I said also, "There are a few from my phalanx who did not make it, and I wish for their bodies to be recovered and brought back inside the Hot Gate."

Before Illi left me, I asked him to have some men recover all the arrows and weapons left on the field. Illi nodded his understanding and asked me how I was. I told him I was fine.

Sari approached me, took my helmet, shield, and spear, and gave me water. I looked at Sari and thanked him.

I told Illi to send a runner to Zee to get a report on injuries and dead from our phalanx. This was done.

I sat down behind the rock wall to rest. I rested as the helots and some of Illi's men exited the gate going onto the battlefield.

As this occurred, Dien approached me and asked, "How did it go out there?"

I told him that the Persians are not used to fighting against our method of warfare. "Stick to the principles of the phalanx and I think we will succeed."

Dien smiled a very rare smile and said to me, "Understood." Dien returned to his phalanx to prepare them to take the field.

After a short time, Illi returned through the Hot Gate with his soldiers and helots. Some were carrying the bodies of our dead. Others were carrying weapons and armloads of arrows.

This process complete, I hollered up to our flute players to signal Dien to take the field. Dien took his phalanx through the Hot Gate and took up his position on the battlefield. The next phalanx had been brought up to the ready position that Dien just vacated. These men were now at rest and receiving water.

My phalanx had been on the field for more than an hour including the arrow attack and the spear combat. I knew that my group would probably have to fight again today. I rested with my eyes closed.

A trumpet sounded from beyond the West Gate. Dom advised me that new troops were marshaling, and I told him by hollering up, "Let me know when they take the field."

The morning breeze had given way to a sunny day. I reflected on the battle. I was proud of my Spartans and the other troops who fought with me. I realized, if I survive this, I would be a changed person. I was now becoming more and more Greek in my thoughts. I still love my Sparta, but I realized that there is a bigger purpose in the form of Greece.

I asked Illi to sit with me. He said he had two things to report to me. He said, "During the arrow attack, we lost three men behind the lines. We were not prepared for the arrows to come over the wall, and before I could give the order to defend against archers, three had fallen and two more were wounded. He said, "One of the men was Spartan."

I asked, "Who?"

"The one you call, Aeros," he responded.

I looked at Illi and asked, "Councilman Aeros?"

Illi nodded and said, "Yes."

I looked at Illi and said, "I should never have brought him here. I will not tell you of the deal I struck with him that let him arrive here with us. I am sorry now I struck the deal. He is the first Spartan to fall. We must return his body to his mother in Sparta."

Illi said, "Our wagons are not going that far for replenishment of supplies."

I responded, "I know a wagon that will go to Sparta."

I left Illi. I walked to the wagons to find Lisee, my beautiful bread maker. She was there with her wagon inside the Hot Gate and saw me approaching. She smiled and asked if I had come to steal more bread.

I told her, "No," and that I have a special request.

She asked me what the request was.

I asked her, "Would you please take the body of Aeros back to his mother?"

She said she would do my bidding. I asked her to leave immediately. She hitched up her horse to her wagon, packed her belongings, and I saw her slowly walk toward Alpeni to retrieve the body of Aeros.

I went back to the wall and joined Dom who was in his ever-observant position and asked what was going on in the Persian camp.

He advised me that new troops had marshaled between our position and the West Gate. They would need to get much closer before he could provide information on the type of troops and their numbers.

I noticed from my position that the ground had become greatly disrupted and muddy due to the battle along with the recent rains.

While standing with Dom, he made a comment to me that took me totally by surprise. He said, "Leonidas, Greece is lucky to have you. Only you could have done what was done here this morning."

I looked at him, nodded acknowledgment and said, "I am going to rest." I climbed down off the wall and sat down beside Sari where he gave me a small meal and more water.

A runner came back from Alpeni with Zee's report that we had lost two Thespians and one fighter from Thebes. He also reported that we had eight or ten minor injuries. He further reported that no Spartans were killed.

I rested. I looked behind me and saw that Kron's men were in resting position with helmets back and shields down.

The phalanx currently on the battlefield has shields that all carry the lambda insignia. The group, that Dien is over, is made up of perioikoi and Spartans.

I am brought out of my thoughts by the sound of trumpets and realize that through the noise above me on the wall, something is happening. I tell Sari to keep my armor nearby as I climbed the wall.

As I arrived, Dom states, "The Persians are taking the field. It looks like they are bringing their very best, the *Immortals*."

I smile at this thought realizing that the Immortals, their very best, would be going up against our very best. Looking down, I noticed Dien had put his men into a loose phalanx in the ready position.

I watched the Persians take the field and realized these may be the only real soldiers Xerxes has. These men will not make the same mistakes that the previous group made. They realize that they cannot fight one hundred across in the confined space of our end of the Pass.

I think about sending a runner down to give Dien some advice, but I realize that Dien is an experienced warrior, and he has at his disposal probably the best group we have here. Dien will use tactics that I am sure will surprise the Immortals.

As I was thinking these thoughts, Dien began moving his phalanx forward at a relaxed pace. I wasn't sure what Dien was up to, but I assumed he had a plan. His phalanx continued to advance until it was at the very edge of the narrow portion of the Pass. At this point, Dien halted the phalanx holding it in ready position.

It is now a little before noon and becoming very hot on the battlefield. I hollered down to Illi that he needs to be prepared because of the troops we are now facing; also, fatigue may cause the need for his men to jump in.

The Immortals are now formed up mirroring our formation of forty across. The only difference is that they are about sixty or seventy deep. I did notice, and I am sure that Dien had noticed, that these men also wear leather armor, leather helmets, and have wicker shields and fairly short spears. At this moment, the groups are facing each other a few hundred feet apart.

By using quick, short commands, many of them actually silent commands, Dien's phalanx closes to *the ready* and brings high and low spears to bear. Without any hesitation, Dien's phalanx starts marching at a rapid pace directly at the enemy. The enemy stands its ground. They are in ranks similar to ours but are not closed up as the ranks of the phalanx are.

Approximately thirty feet from engaging the enemy, Dien, abruptly stops his troops and through commands, rapidly forms his phalanx to eighty across and ten deep. All of a sudden, the Immortals find themselves facing a much wider phalanx.

The Immortals start to advance upon the orders of their captain. As this occurs, the center of the phalanx begins to slowly back-step. The Immortals believe this to be a retreating motion, but this is Dien's Spartan tactic. The entire middle of the phalanx, approximately forty men, is backing up with their backs turned to the enemy. Each flank of the phalanx holds its ground.

Upon seeing the center of the phalanx apparently retreat, the Immortals launched an all-out charge. In doing so, the Immortals broke ranks and started a sprint toward the retreating Greeks.

The slowly retreating center portion of the phalanx still had their backs turned. With a pre-determined command, Dien orders his men to about-face, close the phalanx, turn the left and the right flanks of the phalanx inward, and to begin an advance with low and high spears forward.

Approximately five hundred Immortals are surrounded on three sides by the phalanx now closing in on them. Their only avenue of escape is the way they came.

The first few groups of Immortals engage the phalanx with the same result as the previous battle. The high-low spear attack, as the Greek soldiers move forward, becomes a killing machine. Spears splinter, breaking off spearheads in Immortals' chests, heads, and any body parts reached by the spear. Spears are constantly being passed up as the enemy is slowly engulfed in the three-sided phalanx.

Once it is realized they have walked into a trap, they try to escape. As they do this, they run into the spears of their fellow

Persians. The Immortals, in their attempt to escape, trip over each other and push each other out of the way. Once again, the front lines are running into the back lines creating disorder. They are no longer under the control of their captains. Within a matter of five minutes, over five hundred Immortals are dead.

Upon command, the center of the phalanx catches up to the left and right flanks of the phalanx. The phalanx again is eighty across and begins walking as a group toward the retreating Immortals.

The Immortals never reorganized into a wider formation due to falling into the trap set by Dien in the center of the phalanx. Now, the eighty-man-across phalanx was on the verge of surrounding the rest of the Immortals who were bunched up, one-half trying to come forward and one-half trying to go back. Essentially, the enemy was helping us.

As the phalanx closed on the factions of retreating troops, the Persians were killed with our spears. After one hundred feet, Dien called a halt and an immediate withdrawal to his original position.

I looked at Dom and nodded in the direction of Dien and said, "Another Greek deserving recognition."

Dien's phalanx reorganized in a disciplined manner with the Immortals fully engaged in retreating. As I observed all of this, I could just imagine that Xerxes was furious.

Dien's troops were now on one knee, with helmets up, at rest.

I ordered Illi to send helots out with water. Dien had done a magnificent job of utilizing tactics to defeat a superior numbered force.

The battlefield, once again, became quiet. The battlefield also had become very dangerous with many spears, arrows, and slick mud in the fighting areas.

I told Illi to send a runner out and inquire about injured perioikoi or Spartans. I told him to make sure that reserves went in equal numbers to replace any men brought off the field.

I told Dom to let me know if anything new transpired, and I went down the ladder. I had an idea in my head and had to ask Sari about it.

I found Sari waiting for me at the bottom of the ladder. I asked him if the helots were good bowmen, meaning good archers. I had an idea.

Sari said, "Yes, there are a number of good archers among the helots. They do their hunting with bows." He smiled at me and said, "They are not all just farmers."

I went to Illi and discussed my idea with him about using the helot archers. He saw no problem with doing anything that could provide us with an advantage, no matter how small it could be. I told him that I was still thinking of the details but would make a decision soon.

The battle with the Immortals had been a short one. I decided to leave Dien's troops on the field a little longer in their guard position. They seemed to be resting comfortably and were getting plenty of water.

While at rest, I had little time to think with all the activity around me. I could see Sari would have preferred I return to my tent area, but I told him I could not leave the field.

The day continued to get warmer, and the armor our men wore was hot. For fear of an all-out attack, I hesitated to allow them to remove their armor. Finally, I decided to bring up the next group and recall the perioikoi and Dien's Spartans.

I told Illi to send a runner, and inform Kron that it was time for his group to take the field. Kron was leading a group known as the *Locrians*. The Locrians would be among the first to be overrun if the Pass is turned. I am hoping this is a motivator for them to fight.

I hollered up to Dom on the wall and told him to use the flutes to recall Dien's group. Dien's casualties had already been removed by the reserves. After hearing the orders, Dien brought his group to attention, performed an about-face, and had them march through the Gate.

After this maneuver was completed, Kron, along with his Spartans and the Locrians, took the field. Kron brought his troops into a formation that we had now adopted as our defensive stance. The troops were brought to rest position.

There was still a breeze on the battlefield, and the Spartans and the Locrians stood with their shields on the ground and their helmets pushed back.

During the changeover of forces, more reserves and helots helped clear the field from the previous battle.

I was sure, at this point, that Xerxes was probably furious and frustrated that his best troops were so easily fooled and defeated.

I did now notice that Xerxes's wagon that carried his *high throne* had been moved slightly closer, possibly, to get a better view of the battlefield. I am sure that he noticed, during the previous battles, that we would not engage out on the wide portion of the field. I am sure this is why he moved his perch closer. He stationed guards and a force of men in front of this perch, who were standing in a similar stance to our men, at rest. It wasn't long before flags were posted on Xerxes's perch.

We also heard trumpets in the distance and another group of men beginning to gather. I could see all of this happening by just looking out the Hot Gate. I hollered up to Dom to signal Kron with the flutes to be ready.

I told Illi to get his men assembled and ready to go through the gate at a moment's notice. Illi's force included 100 Spartans; of course, but it also included some Arcadians and some of the Greek States that had provided fewer soldiers. This group had now swelled in numbers including the Spartans to approximately 650 men.

The force that was gathering, approximately one mile away, appeared to be sizable. I had decided to go up on the wall to get a better look at the battle. Once I climbed up, I stood beside Dom.

I glanced over my shoulder to see Gelon bringing his group up and putting them at rest. Our organization seemed to be working out well.

The men who were amassing across from us were taking the entire field of hundreds of feet. They were in long line-like formations too deep to count. I now surmised that Xerxes could not get it done with arrows or his best troops, so he decided to use numbers. Upon hearing trumpet calls, the force started approaching.

Kron had gotten his men into ready position with shields up and helmets down. Unlike Dien, Kron took up his position slightly closer to the wall than Dien's group had been. We were forty across and twenty deep, but the force that was coming toward us could have made those numbers sixty times.

Once I saw the mass of men moving forward, I felt like we would certainly need our reserves. I hollered down to Illi that if his reserves have to take the field, send a runner to tell Gelon to move up to reserve position, and send a runner to bring up Zee's troops.

As the mass got closer, they marched to a strange drum. The drum echoed against the mountain making it seem louder. I feel like the drum was meant to intimidate more than to keep the beat for the men to march to. As before, the enemy group was in a position where they needed to narrow down to get anywhere near us. This disrupted their formations and congested their lines. The center of their group closest to the mountain continued marching forward. They stopped their march when they closed to within one hundred feet.

The Greek phalanx stood firm. As I looked down on the Spartans and Locrians, it was impressive to see the discipline that had been taught and learned over the past week. The Locrians were mirroring the Spartans. Standing in the ready position, there was no movement from any soldier. The blue war cloaks of the Locrians, along with their blue helmet plumes, provided a great contrast to the Spartans' scarlet cloaks and plumes. The sea breeze ruffled the cloaks and plumes as the phalanx stood like stone. It was a Spartan tactic to remain motionless as the enemy approached. By not seeing any emotion or response to their approach, the enemy often became unnerved. It was truly a sight to behold. I silently thanked my captains for their leadership of these soldiers.

The troops that were facing us started a slow measured movement toward us. As they did, the front ranks separated slightly. They were still trying to narrow down to fit in the small confines of this area of the Pass.

At fifty feet, their front line stopped. They held their shields up very high. From my vantage point, I could see they were getting ready to launch some other type of attack.

Before I could send a warning, javelin throwers ran up behind the front line of the enemy that had their shields raised, concealing their activity from the Spartans and the Locrians. Sixty javelins were hurled through the air. While they were still in the air, a second group ran up and threw their javelins followed by a third and fourth group.

Kron gave the command, "Phalanx, DOWN," but the command was a little late.

Some of the Locrians, being new at this maneuver, were slow getting down and getting their shields at the appropriate angle. The end result was javelins penetrated shields, and men cried out in pain.

There were three more volleys of javelins on the way, pinning the Spartans and the Locrians down. We were taking heavy casualties, especially with the Locrians.

After the last volley had been thrown, the force moved forward at a charge running at the front of our formation. Kron heard them coming and ordered, "Phalanx, READY," even though there were still javelins in the air. This was devastating taking out many men including Spartans.

Kron organized the men to tighten the phalanx and move forward to leave behind the injured and dead. As he ordered this, the first Persians arrived, thrusting spears into the shields of the waiting Spartans and Locrians.

The phalanx was somewhat disarrayed and had holes in it that were being penetrated by the enemy. Kron was trying to get the phalanx reorganized but was struggling.

I looked down and ordered Illi to take the field. "Bring your phalanx up behind Kron's group as quickly as possible."

They had to step over many injured and dead men to do this, but the battle was at hand. Illi was in position. The first two lines across were all Spartans.

I told the flute players to order recover. Kron, in the heat of battle, did not hear this.

Meanwhile, Gelon's group moved up to reserve position.

Kron was working feverishly to get his troops organized. With his Spartans, he performed a quick advancing maneuver while attacking high and low on the Persians. By doing this, it gave the troops on either side a break allowing them to re-form.

After a dozen steps forward, Kron did a rapid withdraw to rejoin the phalanx. He passed orders to the left and right for the phalanx to hold.

Kron's group had lost a lot of men, but they were still a viable phalanx. They got stronger as they noticed that there was a second phalanx formed behind them. This restored a sense of calm in the men.

Kron gave the orders for spears and began attacking the enemy. The enemy just kept coming and kept falling. The only way to continue the battle was to take steps forward that were free of bodies. These steps were short and practiced; each stabbing motion was based on a command that had been practiced over and over on the battlefield.

Kron was regaining control of the battle and was still fighting in a confined area of the Pass. The Greek attack continued to the area where the Pass started to widen. At that point, Kron gave the order to extend the phalanx. Even though he had suffered significant losses, he was still able to create a phalanx that was eighty men across. This phalanx was supposed to be ten deep, but through losing so many men, this was no longer possible. Kron's actions prevented any flanking maneuvers by the now, disarrayed Persians.

While this occurred, Illi and his reserves stood behind Kron's men in a loose phalanx. The trouble was Kron could not advance much farther into the Pass. That would leave us open to being flanked. As I observed this from the wall, I knew that Kron would have assessed this by now.

The Persians in the back of their formation had not gotten anywhere near the fighting yet, and already more than one thousand of their troops lay dead. Because they did not know what was happening up front, they kept trying to funnel to the battle scene with this mass of men.

The biggest problem on the battlefield was the bodies that kept piling up. This caused our troops to stumble and trip while trying to advance forward.

Although men up front in the Persian attack were trying to leave the battlefield, they were being pushed back into our spears by their fellow troops. Looking down on the battle from my position, the battlefield on the Persian side looked like chaos.

Kron was now at the edge as far as he could go without having his left flank turned. I fluted down a message to Illi to advance and create a new phalanx to cover Kron's left flank.

We were still taking occasional casualties up front but basically were running the battle our way.

I was not certain that Kron was aware at first that he had help on the field. Word was passed to him from the left flank that the reserves were there. As soon as he heard this, he advanced the phalanx farther into the Pass and began the high-low assault of the phalanx killing machine.

As they moved forward, Illi brought his troops up to the left flank allowing the entire group to fight in a wider portion of the Pass.

The attack now was engaging about one-third of the Persian troops that were on the field. Finally, the Persians were thinning out enough that they could begin to break ranks and successfully retreat.

We were killing 25 or 30 or more men to their one of ours. Finally, we had a phalanx that was amassed 120 across and approximately 8 deep at some points.

The phalanx had gone through many spears. This word was passed up to Kron. Kron halted the phalanx and waited.

The Persians were backing away. Kron recovered his phalanx and began a slow retreat back to the original guard point. At the same time, Illi brought his troops in front of Kron's men forming a phalanx and was also backing up.

During this time, while the phalanx was advanced, I had ordered helots and servants from other city-states out onto the battlefield to dispose of the enemy bodies and recover our wounded and dead.

Kron recovered to his original position. I told the flute to signal him to retire from the field. Kron brought his men to attention, told them to about-face, and marched them through the gate. This had been a true test for the Locrians.

After Kron left the field, the reserves' phalanx backed up into the position that Kron just vacated.

I told Dom to leave the reserves on the field momentarily until we could clear the field a little more.

I then went down to meet with Kron. I told Kron to send his troops to the rear area to recover. I said I would like a report from him on his losses and the losses of the Locrians when he learned this information.

Kron nodded. Before he left, he looked me in the eye and said, "I am sorry I got surprised."

I looked at him and said, "It was easy to see from where I was and very difficult to see from where you were. Get some rest."

It is now mid-afternoon, and I know the fighting is not over. Sari is trying to take care of me, but I tell him, "I have done nothing that requires care at the moment."

Dom reports from the wall that the Persians are clearing some of their dead and wounded from the field.

I sent a runner to bring Gelon to me.

I was trying to think of what Xerxes would do next. He has tried arrows and his best warriors. He has tried a sneak attack using javelins, and he has filled the field with men. This must leave Xerxes very aggravated. As I was having these thoughts, the battlefield was being cleared.

Gelon came to me. I told him, "I don't know what to expect next from Xerxes, but I wouldn't be surprised if it had something to do with horses." I asked him not to advance any farther than necessary into the Pass. "After an advance, retreat back to your original position, and let the enemy pile up if necessary."

Gelon indicated that he understood my instructions.

I hollered up to Dom and instructed him, "Recover the reserves using the flutes." As Illi's troops recover from the field, I call out for him to come and meet with me.

Meanwhile, Gelon marched his troops through the Hot Gate to take up our familiar position. He positioned his men much closer to the wall than the previous two groups. I thought this was a wise decision after the previous battle.

We are now at the hottest part of the day. I tell Illi to rest his troops, but they will stay in reserve.

Meanwhile, Zee has brought his troops up to the ready position.

Gelon is on the field with Corinthians, Arcadians, and his Spartans.

I told Illi that he did a good job. "The surprise attack on Kron's group has cost us. I am waiting for his casualty report."

Illi said that he would get me his report very soon, but that he did not take many casualties.

A runner approached me out of breath. I waited while he recovered. I told Illi to see to his men.

The runner said, "Another group of Arcadians has arrived."

I asked him, "How many?"

He said, "Approximately one thousand."

I told him to bring the Arcadian leaders from both groups to me.

I then went to find Illi. As I did, I looked over at his men who seemed to be in good shape. They were all receiving water and food and resting in the shade of the wall.

Upon finding Illi, I told him of the news of one thousand more Arcadians. I told him that he would need to take fifty of his Spartans, assign them to the new Arcadian group, and Dom would take control of the reserves. I told him to stay with me, as I had sent for both the leader of the original

Arcadian group and the leader of the newly arrived group. The Arcadians promised us these men. It would have been much easier had they come with the original group.

"You are going to have to spend some time with this group to ensure that they are ready to perform as the others. We will not make them fight today as they need to recover from their trip."

Upon the conclusion of this conversation, the two leaders of the Arcadian groups arrived. I told the original Arcadian leader to keep his men in the groups that they already had been assigned to. I introduced the new Arcadian leader to Illi and advised him that his group would fight as a unit. They would have fifty Spartans attached to their phalanx. I explained to the leader, "Illi will be in charge of your phalanx while on the battlefield."

The Arcadian leader agreed.

I turned to Illi and said, "You will take fifty Spartans from our reserve force to embed in the new Arcadian phalanx."

I told the new Arcadian leader, "Since we are fighting in groups of 800 with 50 of the Spartans being embedded in the new phalanx, 250 of your Arcadians will need to be assigned to our reserves under Captain Dom."

I looked at Illi and the two Arcadian leaders and asked if there were any questions concerning my orders. I received no reply and dismissed the group. I instructed Illi and the new leader to make the necessary adjustments for the new phalanx.

I then went up on the wall and advised Dom; he would be taking over the reserves. I advised him to appoint a lieutenant to take over his observation post. Dom nodded his understanding.

At this point, while we were on the wall, there was noise from the West Gate, and once again, we could see men massing to come forward to meet death once more.

I told the flute players to alert Gelon. Gelon immediately brought his men to phalanx ready position with helmets down and shields up.

I also noted, while looking in the distance, I could see some wagons forming up behind the troops. I did not understand this, but the wagons had very high sides; so, whatever they were carrying was being concealed from us.

I told Dom, "Go down and take charge of the reserves." Dom left me on the wall and went to see to his men and get them ready.

Illi had met with his men giving them a quick overview of their assignment and telling them they would get an hour's practice at the end of the battle day. He also instructed 250 of the Arcadians to join the reserve group.

I hollered down to Dom from my position on the wall that the enemy was amassing troops and high-walled wagons. I told him to prepare his men. By assigning 250 of the newly arrived Arcadians, the reserves had been brought up to nearly full strength.

While I was watching the enemy prepare, Dom's lieutenant joined me on the wall, and I instructed him on what his purpose was.

A runner climbed the wall and advised me of the casualty report from Kron. He advised me that the Locrians lost one hundred men and have another fifty men injured. The Spartans lost ten men and have another five men injured. I thanked the runner for his report.

Looking down on the scene toward the East Gate, I observed that Zee had brought his men up. They were receiving water and meals from the many wagons that had been re-positioned between the East Gate and the Hot Gate. I decided, at the end of the day, I would instruct all the groups to bring their camps up so that the distance from the fighting to the rest location would be closer.

The group of Persians in front of Gelon had followed the same tactic as the previous group by moving closer to our position. As they did this, they brought their wagons closer as well.

I signaled down with the flutes instructing Gelon to prepare for a surprise attack involving the wagons. My mind was racing as I was trying to decide how to defeat the wagons. The wagons appeared to be very heavy. They were being pulled by oxen.

I looked at the lieutenant next to me and had my idea. I asked him, "Would you care to dine on oxen this evening?"

He responded, "Yes, King."

I think that Gelon had the same idea; the only way to stop an attack using the wagons was to stop the beasts that were pulling the wagons.

The troops, once again, faced us from one hundred feet away and separated their lines creating gaps in the formation, and I knew what that space would be used for. I believed that they would launch an attack by penetrating our lines using the powerful beasts backed by the weight of the wagons. Those wagons were surely filled with archers or some other men bent on attacking us after breaking through our lines.

Gelon removed the Spartans from the phalanx, forming them into a very tight formation. He instructed the rest of the phalanx to hold.

Gelon waited as he saw the front enemy lines move forward slowly. At the same time, I saw the wagons formed up in groups of three across going several wagons deep. There were more wagons behind them in the distance, but they were not a part of this initial formation. As expected, on a command, the Persians opened their lines allowing the oxen to go through at a rapid rate.

I wondered, *How could they make oxen move so fast?* Three wagons, led by six oxen, were approaching our lines. Each wagon was being pulled by two oxen.

At the fifty-foot mark, Gelon ordered the Spartans to advance at a rapid pace with spears forward, high and low. He kept his formation very tight, and in a few seconds, the Spartan phalanx impacted the oxen leading the way. The animals were impaled with the spears high and low with repeated thrusts bringing them immediately to the ground as they bellowed in pain. As this occurred, the wagons were stopped where they were, and the Pass was essentially blocked.

The Spartans backed the phalanx up ten steps, and after this, Gelon recovered the Spartans back to the original phalanx. The rest of the oxen and carts were jammed and could go nowhere, nor could any of the enemy soldiers advance. Men who had been hiding in the carts were now wondering what their orders were since the plan had failed.

Watching from my position, it was actually a comedy of errors for the Persians. They left themselves no way to effectively retreat, and they had more men on the battlefield than they knew what to do with. Chaos, once again, reigned over the Persians.

The rest of the phalanx stood its ground and waited for the events to unfold. It took the Persians a good forty-five minutes to turn the ox carts and to go back where they had come from through the West Gate. As they did this, one of the carts broke a wheel, was unable to be removed, and was abandoned.

The men who had been in the front carts were, in fact, archers who were wearing no armor and were not interested in being that close to the Spartans and their phalanx. These men exited the carts while the rest of the troops were backing up and leaving the field.

Once it became evident that they were withdrawing, I ordered our phalanx to march forward beyond the carts and to hold position. Gelon accomplished this by having his men go single file between the carts and then reestablish the phalanx.

I advised Dom what had occurred and asked him to send troops out to recover the carts and the animals that we had slain. As this occurred, it was discovered that the carts were filled with arrows. Once we recovered the six dead oxen plus the two live oxen and the four carts, the battlefield was once again clear. Dom did this immediately. It did take a little time with the weight of the oxen, but it was accomplished.

The oxen were taken to our cooks to prepare. At least, we would all eat well tonight.

After the carts and oxen were removed, I had the flutes order Gelon to return to his original position and rest. I somehow felt that we were done fighting for this day.

Just when I thought this, the trumpet sounded again and more men were massing. Gelon saw this and left his men at rest for the moment.

I told the lieutenant next to me to send a runner to Gelon and warn him of a second javelin attack.

I hollered down for Dom to join me for a moment.

I watched the runner approach Gelon and give him this information.

Dom arrived beside me, and I told him my concern. I said, "The only success they have had today is when they tried the javelin attack. They are going to do this again, but this time, they will bring more javelin throwers and try to bring us into the open field first. So, this javelin attack must be stopped before it starts, or we will lose many, many more men."

I instructed Dom to take his reserves out now and fluted Gelon's phalanx a message to advance to a position just before the Pass widened. Dom left the wall and got his men ready. Dom's phalanx followed and came to rest fifty feet behind Gelon's phalanx. The reason for this was to be ready once the attack came.

The word was passed to Gelon that the reserves were coming out. With the addition of Dom's reserves, we now had almost 1600 men on the field. This meant that in a full attack out in the main part of the Pass, we could have 160 across. Both groups now came to rest and waited.

Once again, colorfully dressed Persian troops moved forward to within one hundred feet and stopped. From my observation post, I started to study the ranks of the Persians. I noticed about six ranks back; the men were carrying no shields. I immediately told my lieutenant to leave his position, go down personally and deliver that message to Gelon. He left immediately.

I now knew what would happen. They would engage the front lines of our phalanx with the first few lines of their men. The line of javelin throwers would be concealed behind a line of spearmen with shields who would hold their ground and not move forward and engage the phalanx. Without warning, these javelin throwers would start hurling javelins into the unsuspecting phalanx with devastating effect. I only hoped Gelon knew the plan of how to cope with this issue.

Gelon received the word from our runner. As the runner returned, I could see Gelon passing orders down his line on both the left and right.

No sooner had this occurred than the Persians started advancing slowly. This time, they mirrored our formation in size as they got into the narrower portion of the Pass. This is what we had hoped for.

Our frontline took one step forward disengaging from the phalanx. Once this occurred, what had once been the second line of the phalanx became the front line. The phalanx went to "spears forward, both high and low." The disengaged line of the phalanx did not go to spears but waited in ready position.

None of the Greek phalanx maneuvers were obvious or observable to the approaching Persians. As their line moved closer and closer to the front line of the Greeks, the front separated line took two more steps forward. Just as the Persians were ready to engage, the front line in unison dropped to the ground covering themselves with their shields.

As this occurred, the Persians were confused and stunned to see the phalanx in front of them thrusting spears. They advanced on the phalanx stepping over, or on, the shields to engage the Greeks.

Subsequent lines of the enemy had no idea the Spartan tactic had occurred and charged toward the phalanx that was slowly giving ground backward. The Persians viewed this as an act of retreat paying little attention to the Spartans lying under their shields. After several lines had advanced on the retreating Spartan phalanx, the phalanx stopped backing up and stood its ground.

Following a command, the front line of Greeks who were lying under their shields sprang up with spears forward. They rapidly advanced on the Persians, who were protecting the javelin throwers. This maneuver seemed to stun the enemy, and many of the enemy who were protecting the javelin throwers were immediately dispensed with. The killing continued into the ranks of the javelin throwers. They were now trying to use their javelins in defense with no armor or shields. It was an absolute slaughter of these men. There were rank upon rank of them going down trying to scramble back in retreat, once again, jamming up any further attack by the troops behind the javelin throwers.

At a moment's notice, the attacking Greeks did a disciplined turn facing back toward their own lines and marched with spears forward toward the enemy who was attacking the phalanx. The Persians now trapped between two groups of Greeks. By the time the Persians realized they were totally surrounded, the killing machine was rapidly doing its job.

The main body of the Persians were in disarray and unable to mount an attack due to the retreating javelin throwers.

Meanwhile, the Greeks wiped out the entire front six lines to the man.

The Greeks rejoined the phalanx, once again, forming the front line. Gelon then gave the command for the phalanx to move forward. Dom's phalanx followed.

Gelon had pulled off a very detailed tactical maneuver that saved many Greek troops. He was now leading his men to a wider portion of the Pass to dispense with more of the enemy.

As the Pass started to widen, the Persians turned to make a stand once they recovered from the retreating javelin throwers.

As they advanced into the Pass, Gelon ordered the expansion of the phalanx to eighty across. As the phalanx moved forward, the high-low spears began doing their job. They kept stepping forward until the field expanded more; at which time, Dom brought his phalanx forward to the left flank.

Once the Pass widened further, Dom expanded his phalanx as well. The phalanx that was moving forward now was approximately 160 men across, and at some points, 6 to 10 deep.

From my observations, the phalanx was being operated to perfection. I did see an occasional man fall in our ranks but nothing like the killing that was going on against our enemies.

I looked down at the phalanx and realized that this particular phalanx was made up of Arcadians, Spartans, Corinthians, and Greeks from several other city-states. This was truly a Greek phalanx.

The enemy troops were falling by the hundreds. Their wicker shields and thin armor were no match for our heavy infantry.

Finally, I noticed that spears were getting short, all of the back spears having been passed up. At this point, Gelon halted the advance and called for a slow withdrawal while backing away from the enemy. This was the widest portion of the Pass that we had advanced into during today's battles. Gelon's troops and Dom's were slowly recovering back to their original positions closer to the wall.

From my vantage point, I could see the Persians were retreating. I thought that surely this must be the last attack of the day. It was almost evening.

I turned to the lieutenant next to me and asked his name. He was a Spartan but he was unknown to me. He said his name was Senri.

I said, "Well, Senri, you just witnessed a total coalition Greek force drive back the biggest army in the world and utilize tactics the enemy can't conceive of."

I gave the flute orders for the reserves to leave the field. Once this was done, I gave the orders for Gelon's group to leave the field. I then ordered Zee to the guard position behind the wall, on the wall, and in front of the wall. I told them they would have the guard position for the entire night assuming there were no more attacks.

I sent Senri to talk to Dom and Gelon and get casualty reports. Gelon was taking his troops back in the direction of the East Gate. I felt relieved that we had done it; we had held the Pass for one day. I waited for Senri to return.

Meanwhile, Zee's troops were taking their positions on the wall, in front of the wall, and behind the wall. The helots were busy bringing in our dead and wounded and clearing the field up to the point where it starts to widen.

I climbed down off the wall leaving Zee's guards on duty. Sari provided me some refreshment. I then instructed Sari to go to each group and bring the leaders for a meeting as well as all my captains.

The helots were bringing in the dead and wounded off the battlefield. As they did this, I noticed two of the stretchers were carrying Spartans. I only knew this by seeing their shields and plumes. I decided to walk over. As I did this, I was shocked to see my friend and Captain, Dom, among the casualties. The stretcher bearers stopped. I told them to continue their work.

I quickly made myself go within realizing that Dom did what he was supposed to do and his mission succeeded and that he would be watching the battle from somewhere else now.

Senri reported back to me that fifty Arcadians perished during the battle along with three Spartans.

The captains and the leaders started gathering near the wall and I approached them. I told them that all the troops performed great today. I advised them that we had lost about 163 men, but a number of others had injuries that would prevent them from fighting further. I suggested that these men be taken from the battle area if it was determined that they could no longer fight.

I further reported that we had received one thousand additional troops from Arcadia, and we would be working with them a short time this evening. They would stay as a group and would have fifty Spartans embedded with them under the command of Illi.

"I have promoted Senri to captain to take the place of Dom who fell today. He will be in charge of the reserves."

I also suggested that we move our camp closer to the Phocian Wall so that during rest periods, troops would be closer if needed. Also, they won't have to walk as far to rest. "So, everyone will move their camp inside of the East Gate so that the farthest soldier will only be one-half mile from the Phocian Wall."

The leaders were all quiet. I still had a sense that they were not happy having to relinquish command of their men during the fighting on the battlefield; but had they seen what I saw from the wall, they would have realized the superior tactics that the Spartans were able to bring to bear against the Persians.

I told the leaders and my captains:

I have a plan for tomorrow's battle, and Xerxes is going to help us with our plan. He has provided for us several nice large carts. We are going to use his carts. We have amongst us several hundred helots. They have amongst them some absolutely great archers. We have acquired, thanks to Xerxes, thousands of arrows.

The helot bowmen are going to be part of a two-pronged attack. At first light, we will push the carts that they gave us out into the Pass. We will protect these carts from the front with our phalanx. We will fill these carts with archers. These archers will have the onboard equipment to create flaming arrows. I feel the flaming arrows will do well with the wicker shields.

On our wall, we will have additional archers who have told me that they can fire their bows several hundred feet. We will put that to the test tomorrow. These arrows, from the archers on the wall, will add to the surprise. Make no mistake, tomorrow's fighting will be worse than today's.

Xerxes will not settle for what has occurred. I am sure that his captains are paying the price for not taking the Pass.

A leader from Corinth asks, "How can we keep this up day after day?" I looked at him. I said, "We have no choice. We cannot desert the Pass. We have proven today, even against his best soldiers, they are no match for our armor or tactics. The practice you received here is keeping your men alive. It could have been a lot worse today. The enemy losses today were in the thousands. Remember, we are all Greeks. If you have not decided that by now, then you are in the wrong camp. I consider you all my brothers. I have fought beside you and your men. I am taking my turn in battle." No more was said.

I looked at the leaders and said, "Except for some of the supply wagons, move the camp to within one-half mile of this wall. Also, we must post a guard at the east end in case something happens and the path through the mountains is turned. We do not want to get surprised from behind. Move your men; and then, we will feast on the eight oxen that were provided to us by Xerxes."

The meeting breaks up. I tell Sari, "Move my tent up front to within one hundred feet of the Phocian Wall. I need to be close to the battle." I also instruct Sari to get me a spokesperson for the helot bowmen. Sari leaves.

I go over to the area where the reserves are grouped about one hundred yards from the wall. They gather when they see me come over, all seven hundred or so of them. I address them and thank them for the job they did today and for the quick response to help their fellow Greeks.

I then told them that Senri had been chosen by me and promoted to captain to replace Dom. I said, "Senri will be a good captain. Follow his orders and you will be successful." I observed many nods of the affirmative and left the group.

Away from the group, I spoke with Senri. I advised him, "Fill the openings in the rest of the phalanxes to replace the men who have fallen today. I know that will deplete your reserves somewhat, but we need to keep our main phalanx groups at full strength." Senri nodded his understanding.

I went to the area where I wanted my tent set up and sat down on the Earth and relaxed. I was now alone with my thoughts; at least, I thought I was.

I noticed in the distance, the tents were being set up, and many more wagons were being moved in. I also noticed that the Arcadians were taking the field a good distance away to receive instructions from Illi on maneuvers of the phalanx. Unfortunately, the fifty Spartans who were embedded with them had to practice, as well, even though they had already fought today.

A short while later; Sari arrived with my tent and belongings. He was accompanied by a small helot who was rather old. Sari introduced him as "Hemi." He said, "Hemi is the leader of the bowmen and makes many of the bows they use."

I told Hemi to sit with me while Sari set up my camp. I explained to Hemi how I intended to use the bowmen. He seemed genuinely interested and excited about participating in the battle.

I told him, "At first light, have your archers ready at the Hot Gate. Your best long-range archers need to be posted on the wall. We have plenty of arrows for them."

He asked, "Will my men in the wagons be protected?"

I said, "Yes, you will be protected by a phalanx, and when it is time to withdraw, you will exit the wagons and retreat from behind our phalanx."

He nodded his understanding, and I told him that he needed to get his men ready for tomorrow. Before I dismissed Hemi, I instructed him, "After you explain what your men are to do, take them to the feast on my orders. If you will fight with the rest of the Greeks, you deserve to be treated like Greek soldiers."

He looked at me and said, "Thank you, King," bowed slightly and walked away.

Sari had completed my tent. I told him I would rest and take my meal later.

I looked around at the area in the direction of the East Gate. Our new camp was taking shape rapidly. I also noticed the many cooking fires and preparations for roasting the oxen Xerxes has so generously provided. Troops were mulling around and interacting with each other instead of just staying within their city-states. I got the sense by observing this, that it was more than just me who was becoming a Greek.

The only downside to our situation was the increasing odor of the dead. I instructed our helots to only dispose of Persians who blocked our immediate area where we chose to fight. The rest of the field was up to the Persians to clear. They were slow to do this. There were still hundreds and hundreds of bodies on the battlefield, and the smell was becoming a problem.

I went back to my tent to rest. I told Sari, "Don't let me be disturbed unless it is important."

He nodded and I went to my tent to seek the solitude it offered. I rested and thought about Dom. I had not been with him when he perished in battle nor did I see him go down. He was a trusted soldier and friend, and I realized that I could not bring him back. The best I could hope for was to make his death count for something.

I realized I had been on the wall much of the day and fatigue was setting in. I slumbered out of exhaustion.

It seemed like I had only slept a short time when Sari woke me telling me that a runner had come with a message. He was a seaman and was reporting on the battle of our navy. I listened to his report, and he let me know our flank to the right was not to be turned. I thanked him for his report and advised him to express that all Greeks fought in the Pass today and we, as well, held. He nodded and was off with my message.

Before I could go back to my tent, Sari insisted I needed to eat. I looked out over the camp and heard the sounds of laughter and people enjoying themselves with a good meal.

Sari brought me food from the feast, which I graciously ate. While I was sitting at my fire, I looked at Sari and asked him to sit and join me. He looked at me with bewilderment.

I told him, "You brought enough food to feed three kings. I insist you dine with me."

Sari smiled and said, "With pleasure."

There comes a point, where sometimes, friendship and caring for others overrides one's station in life. So Sari and I sat together, Master and servant, dining together.

As we were dining quietly, Senri approached us. I looked at him, and he asked if he could have a word. Sari started to get up, and I held his arm to hold him back down.

I looked at Senri and said, "Sari is a most trusted friend and will not speak of anything you say here." Upon hearing this, Sari looked at me, and I could see in his eyes that our bond was unbreakable.

Senri took my words for fact and I instructed him to sit with us. I offered him dining, but he stated he had already eaten. I felt like I knew what was on his mind. Before he could start, I said to him, "You are questioning your command."

He looked at me and said, "I am Sir."

I told Senri:

> My choice for this command was not made by me; it was made by your Captain Dom. You were good enough in his eyes and that is all I need to know.

> Tomorrow, you will fight; you will lead the Arcadians and the other reserves from all the city-states who have sent smaller numbers of troops. Your group of reserves contains more different Greek city-states than any other group here. Our forces have soldiers from over fifteen locations, some large cities and some small villages. You are the only thing some of these men have to look up to.

> Some of them came here with nothing more than a spear, and we provided them with the shield and a helmet. They were not soldiers; they were farmers or carpenters or some other trade. They are now soldiers under your command. So, go forward tomorrow and honor your Captain and me.

Senri looked at me with new eyes of understanding. I concluded our meeting by telling him, "You are the best man for this job at this hour." Senri got up, thanked me for the meeting, nodded to Sari and left.

Sari looked at me and said, "Greece is lucky to have you."

I told Sari, "I better rest now because tomorrow will certainly be no better than today."

Before I could do this, another runner came. Gelon had spoken with each of the other captains and spoken with our medical people. He reported, "Of the approximately one hundred injured, twenty-five of them had passed, and several who were too serious to continue fighting have been sent back with supply wagons." I nodded at this information and thanked him.

I told Sari I would try to rest some more and went into my tent as the camp got quiet.

Late in the night, I heard a commotion near the Phocian Wall. I could hear a call to arms, and I immediately left my tent and found Sari at my side.

I told Sari, "Get my helmet, shield, and spear." He insisted on carrying them for me as we walked toward the Hot Gate.

The activity had mustered Zee's phalanx. As I approached, they were forming up on our side of the Hot Gate. I came upon Zee and asked about the situation.

He said, "Our lookout is on the wall, and he passed a signal by runner to our men in front of the wall that intruders were approaching."

The group on guard at the time was the Spartans which numbered fifty. "Several Spartans were spread out in a guard position away from the wall in the area where we form our phalanxes. These guards were the first to engage the Persian assault group. The rest of the Spartans were in the shadows of the wall and undetected and unseen by the assailants. The assailants numbered twenty-five men. They overpowered the three Spartans that were the lead guards. The forty-seven remaining Spartans launched an all-out charge with spears forward in a disciplined line, with a reserve line, and dispensed with the assailants in very short order. It was all over in two minutes. We did capture one assailant whose injuries are minor. Fearing that this may be a prelude to a larger attack, I mustered the rest of my phalanx."

I looked at Zee and told him to double the guard in front of the wall and keep his men "at the ready." Because they will be up all night, they will not be the phalanx who takes the field at first light.

Zee nodded his understanding and instructed fifty Thespians to take the field in support of the Spartans.

I climbed the ladder to the wall. On top were several Thespians posted, and I looked down and into the darkness but could not see the activity going on below.

I left the wall and went out the Hot Gate. As I did, I received an escort of ten Thespians. I turned and looked at them and decided to leave well enough alone and accepted the escort. I walked to the field and once again found Zee. The Thespians had taken up a position in a loose phalanx, ten across and five deep in our normal set-up location.

Zee looked at me and reported, "Three more Spartans have fallen." I took this news with regret.

I asked about the raider they had captured. I said to Zee, "Interrogate this man and learn all you can."

Zee did say, "They carried equipment to climb the wall and archery equipment to subdue any guards on our wall.

They were clearly trying to gain access to assassinate you, King. You must let us post guards at your tent."

"I already have an assigned bodyguard." I told Zee, "Let me know the results of your interrogation."

Zee argued, "Those bodyguards are now going to live in your camp." I nodded my understanding and left.

I went back through the Hot Gate followed by the ten Thespians. They stayed at the gate as I walked back to my camp.

Sari was with me on my walk back, and I looked at him and said, "I guess I won't need my armor tonight." Sari made no comment.

I went to my tent area and sat by the fire that Sari was building. Soon thereafter, my ten Spartan bodyguards arrived, came to attention and stated that they were ordered to guard my camp.

I looked at them and said, "Who ordered you?"

They stated, "Captain Zee."

I told them, "Follow your orders." In sitting there, I did not feel the need for the bodyguards, but I respected the wishes and wisdom of my captain.

After about an hour, Zee came to my camp and advised that the interrogation was complete. He informed me, "The Persian was assigned, in fact, to seek you out and kill you." He also said that the Spartans you sent to attack Xerxes were killed.

I now knew I had thirty more names to add to my list. I thanked Zee for his report and told him to go back to his men.

I sat there wondering what more I could do. I thought about my idea of the archers, but I wondered what great effect it would actually have.

I called to Sari to ask him a question. He stopped what he was doing, and I asked, "Are there any good javelin throwers among the helots?"

He smiled. He replied, "Great King, you know we are not allowed to practice throwing javelins."

I looked at him and smiled. I said, "I need some men who can climb the cliffs overlooking our position. The same men must be able to throw javelins. Quite possibly, we can surprise Xerxes one more time."

Sari smiled and said he would see what he could do. He left immediately and I was alone with my bodyguards and my thoughts.

I looked at the lead bodyguard and asked his name.

He said, "I am Gallus."

I realized that when we chose the men for this mission, the most important part was to have the right captains. I allowed them, in turn, to fill the ranks with the right men. I knew some of the men but not all.

I waited for Sari to return. I wondered if we could hold tomorrow like we held today. The battlefield was getting messy as well as smelly. I realized that I could only control what my men do and not what the enemy does.

Sari arrived back at camp with Hemi. And apparently, Hemi knew of several helots who had great abilities with the javelin. He told me, "If they were allowed to participate in the Olympics, they would win with distance and accuracy."

I smiled at this. I asked him, "Do you have ten such men, and can they climb cliffs?"

He said, "They could climb the cliffs a little farther in but could not climb closest to the wall."

I told him that we had acquired many javelins, and we could provide his men with those javelins. If his men could climb the rocks above the battlefield, they would be able to throw at the groups of attacking Persians with their choice of targets. The problem is, once their ammunition ran out, they would be exposed to possible enemy archers.

My plan was this: to station ten javelin throwers at the earliest point on our end of the Pass where the mountain could be climbed. Once there, these men could conceal themselves among the rocks and crevices. They could begin their assault once the Persians approached. Once they ran out of ammunition, we would push forward to a point to allow them to come down off the rocks and escape behind our left flank.

"How does this sound, Hemi? Before first light, send your ten men to Zee. Zee will have your javelins tied together in bundles for you to carry up the cliffs. This must be done before light. Tell your men to not wear anything bright so they may blend in with the rocks. If the Persians do see them, their first thought will be that they are observers."

Hemi nodded.

I told Hemi, "We will use the archers in the second phalanx, not the first one."

I looked at Spartan Gallus of my guard and asked him to send a runner to get Captain Zee. This was done immediately.

Hemi left without further words.

A few moments later, Zee arrived with the runner. I explained to Zee my plans for the javelin throwers. I told him to have the javelins packaged and ready for them before dawn.

He nodded and I dismissed him.

I asked my new personal Spartan guard to advise Captain Illi that he would be the first phalanx in the morning. He nodded his understanding and ran to wake my captain with this message.

I retired to my tent to get a few hours of sleep. I went to bed feeling there was nothing more that I could do. I had taken all the resources that Xerxes had sent me: his arrows, his javelins, his carts, and the great meal of oxen.

I called to Sari to wake me before light. He acknowledged.

I lay awake wondering how the day would go tomorrow and what new challenges we would face. We had all done well today. The Spartans had fought well in their leadership role, and the rest of the Greeks held firm. All-in-all, it could not have gone much better.

Exhaustion set in and I slept.

CHAPTER ELEVEN

THE GREEK WALL

Eighth Day at Thermopylae

The Greek flag will take the day. Thermopylae will remain Greek soil, but the mothers of Greece will mourn the many who perish.

Although it seemed I had only rested for moments, I guessed as many as five hours had gone by when Sari woke me. I was tired but felt the pressure of my job in the understanding that I must be visible for the rest of the men to do their job.

I told Sari I was going to the Hot Gate to see the helots off on their mission.

He nodded and said a meal would be waiting for me when I got back.

As I started for the Hot Gate, I looked over my shoulder to find my ever-present guard walking a short distance behind me. I was too tired to argue with them, so I allowed them to perform their duties.

When I approached the Hot Gate, the helots had already arrived and were being organized and assisted with the batches of javelins. The javelins had been strapped together in bundles.

Zee addressed me explaining that a detachment of his men was going to accompany the helots to the cliffs that they would be climbing. The javelins would then be passed up by rope. Zee explained that we would be utilizing some of the rope equipment that we confiscated off the raiding party from the night before.

I looked at the helots and told them, "Hold your positions. Stay as hidden as possible. You will know when to launch your missiles. Keep throwing until you are out of javelins. Then wait. If the phalanx is not close by, it will advance so you can come down and retreat safely."

The men looked at me and said that they would do their best.

I did tell them, "I will not forget this service you are providing us." At that point, they departed through the gate into the darkness with an escort of thirty Spartans.

I looked at Zee and told him, "Let me know when the men are in place. At first light, the reserves will resume their position relieving your men from their current duty. Because you had extended duty and disarmed a conflict the previous night, the other four phalanxes will go into battle before your group fights again."

Zee nodded his understanding and we parted without further words.

I returned to my tent and received some nourishment from Sari's cooking. It was still a good hour before light, but I told

Sari to fetch the reader and bring the sacrifice. He left immediately.

I knew today would be worse than yesterday. I did not need any sacrifice or reader to tell me this. This is information I knew through my experience as a field general.

Once Sari returned, the reader was accompanying him carrying a chicken. I told the reader; he would have to do his reading by torchlight because I could not wait for the coming day.

He nodded in understanding.

I dispatched the chicken and handed it to Megis. He studied the chicken using the glowing light from our torch. He turned to me and said, "The Greek flag will take the day. Thermopylae will remain Greek soil, but the mothers of Greece will mourn the many who perish."

I accepted the omen. The reader departed without further comment.

I told Sari to go wake all my captains and the various leaders for a meeting. He left immediately.

I had set the plan in motion, and I hoped this tactic would further disrupt Xerxes and his men.

I waited for some long minutes as the captains and leaders of the Greek troops slowly arrived at my tent area. I bid that they all sit down and relax because today would be a long day. Everyone had shown except for Zee.

I decided to go ahead with my meeting. I explained the order that the phalanxes would fight in today with Illi's phalanx being first, Dien's being second, Kron's being third, and Gelon's, fourth. I advised the group about the trouble the night before and that Zee's guard was forced to remain on alert the entire night. I said, "Because of this, they have been moved to the fifth phalanx position."

I explained that we had two surprises today for Xerxes. "The first is our javelin assault from the cliffs, which will occur during the first phalanx. The second is to utilize the wagons that we captured by filling them with archers as well as placing archers on the wall during the second phalanx."

The leaders accepted these plans with enthusiasm. All of them seemed to show a little more resolve than we had the day before.

I let them know that our reserves had grown in numbers as new volunteers entered our camps. I reported to them that the total fatalities from the first day were 188 men with approximately 100 injured. I followed up, "Last night, we lost 3 more Spartans and we learned that our attempt at attacking Xerxes from behind using the path with 30 Spartans has failed." I then asked if any of the leaders had any comments or reports.

The leader from Malis advised that he heard reports that some of the men had deserted during the night. This report did not shock me. I already knew that few of the Greek defenders were actually soldiers. After such a long day, and seeing some of their fellow citizens fall, I anticipated there would be some desertions.

I told the group, "I have already ordered that your injured and dead be replaced by reserves. In addition, take account of your men, and we will also fill your deserted positions. That is what the reserves are for."

The Thespian leader asked if we had heard any information from the Phocians who guarded the path defending our rear.

I advised them that I had not received any word. The only report that I had received was, "The sea battle and the defense of our right flank is going well in favor of the Greeks."

I then told them the reading of the day and explained to them, "Greece will win the day, but it will cost us dearly."

I could detect many grim expressions reflected in the torchlight. I said, "Stick to the principles of your phalanx. Do not allow it to be turned, and remember, the reserves will come in if you need help." I asked if there were any further questions. There were no comments or words.

I advised the leaders and my captains, "It is time to go to work." I told Illi to stay behind. I told Senri to bring his reserves up and relieve Zee's group.

After everyone had left, I advised Illi that I would fight with his group and to leave a place in the second line beside him. Illi nodded his understanding.

I then asked Illi how the Arcadians would do. He expressed that they took to the training very well and spent two hours practicing what they would need to know in the phalanx.

I nodded my understanding and told Illi I would see him at the Hot Gate at daylight.

I then noticed that the whole camp was waking up and moving around. Campfires were lighting, and the smell of food cooking was permeating the air. We were now about thirty minutes from daylight.

I received a runner from Zee advising that the helot javelin throwers were in place and well concealed high above the battlefield. I thanked the messenger but offered no reply. He left immediately.

After a quick meal, I told Sari to get my armor. While I was preparing for battle, I wondered if this would be the day a king of Sparta would die. I was not comforted that my first battle of the day would be surrounded by "green" troops from Arcadia, but I realized I had put this same dilemma on the rest of the Spartans by splitting them among the various phalanx groups. I finished with my armor and Sari accompanied me carrying my helmet, shield, and spear as we walked to the Hot Gate.

Senri's reserves had relieved Zee's phalanx and taken up the guard position on the outside of the wall, on the wall, and behind the wall.

Since all the new troops had arrived, there were many city-states represented within the reserves. The largest portion, however, remained Arcadians.

I found Senri and asked him how the situation looked. He said that his spotters on the wall have seen no sign of enemy activity. The sun was just coming up.

No sooner had this conversation occurred, when a call came down from the wall that a rider was approaching. The rider stopped just beyond our guard that was stationed outside the wall. The word was passed that the rider was asking for the king.

I immediately went through the Hot Gate followed by my escort. As we went through the Hot Gate, I turned and instructed them to stay back. They continued to accompany me onto the battlefield but remained a good twenty paces behind me.

Fifty Arcadian soldiers were on outside guard duty and in guard-ready position. I walked just beyond them and hailed the rider, "What do you want?"

He stated, "Xerxes admires your fighting ability and wishes to offer his final opportunity for you to surrender. I am awaiting your words."

I turned behind me and looked at the Arcadians. I looked at them, left and right in their ranks, and I said to them, "Are you ready to become Persians?" There was no answer.

I turned to the emissary and said, "We do not accept your offer to surrender." I turned and walked away from the emissary. I could hear his horse leaving and galloping away. I just hoped that the emissary had not looked up and seen our helot surprise that we had stationed on the cliffs.

I walked back through the Arcadian guard and back through the Hot Gate.

I advised Senri to keep plenty of runners ready on the wall today and man the wall himself for observations of enemy activity. I told him to use the soldier Gallus as his second on the wall.

He stated, "This will be done."

I climbed the ladder to the wall followed by Senri. I told Senri that Illi's phalanx would be taking the field momentarily. I explained to him, "Since many of the reserves are Arcadians, they should be very willing to jump in if their fellow citizens get in trouble."

I advised Senri to send runners down or send us a flute signal if they detect something on the battlefield from their position on the wall.

I looked behind me and saw that phalanx one made up of Arcadians and Spartans was preparing to take the field. I noticed behind them, phalanx number two made up of perioikoi and Spartans was formed up and prepared to move into the ready position.

With a loud noise of trumpets, my attention was then drawn to the other end of the Pass. Troops could be seen gathering on the field in the distance. I knew it would not be long now before this day's battles would begin. We waited.

Senri and I watched as the mass of men grew larger and larger taking up much of the width of the Pass and moving forward across the field. I sent a runner to tell Illi and phalanx one to take the field. This was done without hesitation.

I told Senri to use the flutes to withdraw his Arcadian guard behind the wall. I restated, "After phalanx one takes the field, get the reserve phalanx lined up and ready to go through the gate at a moment's notice."

Senri nodded.

I looked down to see Dien climbing the ladder to the wall. I looked at Dien waiting for an explanation. He stated, "Once the first phalanx moves up, my phalanx has been instructed to move to the ready position. I thought that my eyes could be of better use to you up here as opposed to standing or resting with my men."

I nodded in agreement.

During this conversation, Senri had recalled his Arcadian guardsmen back within the Hot Gate. Instantly, Illi was taking his phalanx out onto the field. I could see, once again, the familiar formation of forty across and twenty deep in ready position. Illi then brought the phalanx to rest on the battlefield.

Looking at the enemy, who was now marching toward us less than one-half of a mile away, I wondered what trickery Xerxes was planning for this attack.

Our reserves were stationed and ready inside the Hot Gate. Phalanx two with the perioikoi and Spartans had moved up and were staged to go out next. I then noticed phalanx three; the Locrians and Spartans had formed up behind phalanx two and was seated and resting.

I turned my attention to the battlefield. It appeared that the Persian attack was being led by yet another group of colorfully dressed tribesmen carrying small wicker shields and short spears. Their ranks were spread way out. I was wondering if they had not learned anything from yesterday. It probably unnerved them somewhat to see a small group of Greeks calmly standing and waiting for them to arrive.

There were now more men on the enemy side of the battlefield than could be counted. It's as if Xerxes gave the order to fit as many men into the Pass as possible. This was a poor general's decision in my opinion.

As the enemy troops grew nearer, I saw no such threats as I had in the previous day. I could detect no hidden javelin throwers or archers.

I told Senri to go down and join up with his troops as I was going out to join my phalanx. I asked Dien to stay on the wall. Senri went down the ladder followed by myself.

Sari handed me my helmet, shield, and spear and wished me well. I walked out the Hot Gate and went to the front of the formation and found my position next to Illi. I relieved one of the Spartans who was instructed to go back behind the wall.

I walked out in front of the phalanx, turned to the men, and addressed them, "Greeks! Orders for the day: hold the phalanx, move forward on my command. We will have some help from the rocks above; after this occurs, we will advance."

No comment was made. I raised my spear over my head and uttered the words as loudly as I could, "Greece!"

The men of my phalanx began the chant mirroring my upheld spear, and the chant *Greece* was eventually being echoed from the eight hundred voices against the walls of the Pass. A rhythmic *Greece, Greece, Greece,* resounded.

I re-entered the phalanx and ordered the preparatory command, "Phalanx" followed by the command of execution, "READY." The Persians kept marching closer and closer. As they approached our end of the Pass, where it narrowed, they were forced to bunch up. The men approaching us appeared to have no armor, just a small shield.

Once they were as close as fifty yards, the front ranks of these men broke into a sprint toward our lines. The front portion of the Persians was now well within striking distance of our javelin throwers up on the cliffs.

The men that were sprinting toward us would run into a wall. I gave the order, "Phalanx, HOLD."

The phalanx was braced as tight as it could be from our closed formation with the shield of the man behind me pushed up against my back. The wall was now set as it started being peppered with men running into it. I think that these men were surprised that they could not run through our wall. As they ran into it, they basically bounced off and many tumbled to the ground tripping other soldiers as they arrived. Eventually, so many men were jammed into such a small space that the charge was stalled by their own inept tactics.

At this very moment, I began to hear screams and cries from deep into the enemy lines. I could only imagine that our javelin throwers were having success without having to work at picking a target. The screams continued.

I gave two consecutive orders. I ordered the phalanx to step back to disengage from the enemy while going to all spears position. I followed this with the orders, "Phalanx, ADVANCE; Phalanx, ATTACK." This resulted in the phalanx steadily moving forward while thrusting with high and low spears. This caused the immediate demise of enemy troops who came in contact with our phalanx.

I could only imagine what was going on in the enemy ranks with javelins raining down on them while we were depleting their front lines. Subsequent lines were witnessing all of this.

I decided between thrusts that Xerxes had probably filled the field with men to prevent a retreat. We continued moving forward stepping on and over bodies of those we had just killed. The cries and screams and splintering wood spears resounded along the front. It had become hard to step over or on so many bodies that were now congesting the small area of the Pass.

The men, who had attacked us, were filled with spirit but did not have any protection from our weapons. In any case, they still achieved some small successes by thrusting their short spears under our shields. This caused some of our front-line ranks to fall who were quickly replaced by the men behind them.

The phalanx moved forward as planned. It was very slow going because the mass of men in front of us could only stand or be killed. They had no opportunity to retreat.

I felt that we needed to advance and expand our phalanx to the full eighty-man front to allow our helots on the cliffs to be able to come down and escape. This battle was becoming intense and horrendous with such a mass of humanity: half of it living and half of it dying. Before we had gone fifty feet, I was already on my third spear.

Also, Illi had moved up to the front line due to the man in front of him falling. I did not have time to glance up and down the lines, but it seemed like the Arcadians were holding.

As the phalanx moved forward ever so slowly, I gave the order to expand to its full width. As the Pass widened, so did our phalanx. At the most, some of our lines were only seven or eight deep. As we spread out the phalanx, we prevented any flanking maneuvers. On the right flank, the preferred method of killing the enemy was to impale them and twist the spear slightly so that they would fall off the cliff. So, it was somewhat easier going on the extreme right flank due to the assistance of the cliff.

After about twenty-five minutes of fighting, we had achieved a location that would safely allow our helots to escape behind our lines. I was now able to glance up and see them throwing one javelin after another. They had taken enough javelins up so that each man had one hundred javelins to throw. I am sure their arms were getting tired by now, but they did not have to worry about accuracy. Throwing the javelins into the mass of enemy troops created little opportunity to miss.

The helots were now finishing up their ammunition and scrambling down the rocks to safety, and our phalanx was still working to perfection; however, the phalanx was tiring. I hoped Dien could see this, and would bring up the next group. We fought on, but I knew the Arcadians were not conditioned for this long a fight.

I ordered a slow withdrawal in which the enemy followed. I would halt the withdrawal every so often to thrust spears high and low to keep masses of the enemy from having an effect on our withdrawal. I then heard flutes behind me signaling that another group was on the field behind us.

I ordered the phalanx to recover to our original forty-across, twenty-deep formation. I then ordered the front two lines to hold as the rest of the phalanx made a rapid withdrawal. After one minute of withdrawal, I ordered the front two lines to retreat while maintaining their shields in ready position. This retreat was very difficult because we were constantly stumbling over bodies. The enemy was relentless and was charging our retreat.

Dien's group was moving forward to cover our withdrawal. His phalanx was set with forty across and twenty deep, turned sideways, to allow our phalanx to escape behind them.

A few of our men had tripped and were covered by the enemy immediately. Our withdrawal finally made it to Dien's group and was now behind the protection of his phalanx.

Phalanx one was now heading behind the Hot Gate to recover. As I went through the Hot Gate, Sari found me; took my helmet, spear, shield, and gave me a drink. I thanked him and climbed the ladder.

On top of the wall, I found Kron observing the battle. I also noticed that his troops had been brought up into the ready position, and behind them, phalanx four with the Corinthians was being brought up by Gelon.

The battle scene that I look down on is chaotic, but I now have the best group on the field that I could possibly have. Dien was faced with the same situation we had just had except the battlefield was almost a solid mass of dead soldiers before him. This meant that as the Persians attacked, they were standing on the bodies of their fallen. This fact created a slight advantage to the Persians raising them up a number of inches in height, but Dien's phalanx held firm giving no ground. Dien's soldiers were fighting on solid ground, and the enemy soldiers were walking into the spears.

As the bodies built up, Dien utilized a new tactic by having the phalanx step back five steps. When this occurred, the enemy would climb over the mound of dead. Then Dien would move forward attacking offering no retreat to the new Persian attackers. They were trapped between a wall of spears and a mound of dead soldiers. This occurred three or four times.

The Persians in reserve were unable to negotiate the pile of bodies that was, in some cases, three or four high to launch any type of attack. They were unable to have any footing, therefore, were totally ineffective against Dien's phalanx.

The attack from the Persians finally subsided, word getting back that the Pass was too blocked with bodies to continue pushing forward. Dien noticed this and brought his men to rest position.

I hollered down and instructed Senri to send out one hundred of his men and some helots to clear the initial battlefield, and recover our wounded and dead. Senri did this instantly.

In the distance, I could see the Persians regrouping and I thought, *We needed to give them a reason to withdraw to rethink their strategy.*

I ordered the wagons and the helot archers to the gate. They had been standing by waiting for this order. Once the battlefield was cleared for one hundred feet ahead, we would push the wagons out and position our phalanx in front of them. We would begin the next battle in a wider phalanx but would have the four wagons filled with archers and thousands of arrows waiting.

The helots and Senri's men made quick work of clearing the field by throwing the bodies of the Persians over the cliff. All of our dead and wounded were recovered behind our lines. I sent a runner down to tell Dien what we were going to do.

Once Senri's men had recovered inside the Hot Gate, I instructed that the wagons be pushed onto the field. Upon hearing the wagons approach, Dien marched his phalanx forward and spread it out to the full eighty-man front. The wagons were pushed up behind them and the group came to rest. There were about ten archers in each wagon with thousands of arrows at their disposal. There was a calm over the battlefield at the moment.

I asked a runner to go find the helot Hemi. Hemi was brought to me a short time later. Hemi came up the ladder. I asked him how it had gone, explaining that being in battle, I was unable to see the effect of his javelins.

Hemi smiled and said, "There were many targets and one could have been blind and not missed a target." He felt that at least one man was taken down with every throw of the javelin.

From the field, I could not see the effect of this, but it did have an effect. Also, when the Persians who were being hit with the javelins tried to retreat, they were stopped and some were even being killed by their own men.

Hemi looked at me and said, "What kind of leader kills his own men who are trying to flee danger?"

I just smiled. I put my hand on his shoulder and thanked him for his service.

He smiled, left and went down the ladder.

I told Senri, "Keep your men at-the-ready because the phalanx on the field was beginning in a more extended position."

I looked at Kron and said, "I hope the Persians think we are using the wagons to allow us to have a wider phalanx." Kron made no comment.

I told Kron to send a runner to get a casualty report from Illi's phalanx.

Looking in the distance, the Persians actually never left the field. They were back about a mile from our location but had decided, apparently, similar to ourselves, to bring more men up and operate closer to the battle area.

I also noticed that the rolling platform to provide Xerxes a view of the battle had been moved up much closer as well. A thought occurred to me. If we had enough men, we could meet them in the open field with a massive phalanx and drive them into the tiny West Gate. Possibly, we could capture or kill Xerxes during such a battle. But, we did not have a sufficient number of men to do this.

My thoughts were interrupted by the sound of trumpets yet again, and this time, long lines of men started moving forward approximately one-half of a mile away. I stood in observation waiting to see what Xerxes would try next. They had not cleared their dead from the battlefield, and we were not about to do it for them.

As the men approached, they were in five distinct lines. I told Kron to send a message to Dien; it looked like archers were once again going to come into play.

The archers in our wagons were well protected behind thick wood and only needed to stay down. I counted one line of over one hundred men and assumed that the other lines were equal. We were getting ready to face an attack by over five hundred archers.

I then made a decision. I told Senri, "Take your reserves to the field. Extend the phalanx and get the archers off the field." Senri complied with this order.

I sent a runner to pass this information on to Dien. We would now move forward to a position with 160 across and 10 deep.

It took Senri's men less than two minutes to go out the gate and form up. Dien then marched his troops forward to allow for the additional phalanx.

I looked down at the beautiful sight of seeing a Greek phalanx of 160 across and 10 deep in most places. The wagons stayed in place, and the helots stayed hidden for use later in the battle.

Dien and Senri's men had marched as far as they could without giving up a flank; however, their intention was to drive the archers from the field. To do this, they would need to do a rapid advance.

The archers were in lines separated by several feet. They were steadily approaching the phalanx. They knew they could not be effective against the Greek armor from any distance. Once they closed to about two hundred feet, they were beginning to prepare their attack. They were probably happy that we had pulled out of the narrow part of the Pass and were now preparing to engage them in the open field.

As the first archers prepared to fire, Dien and Senri, both gave orders for a full charge against this enemy with the entire combined phalanx. This charge was made with shields raised at a forty-five-degree angle.

The front line of the Persians saw they were being charged and brought their bows down to a straighter trajectory. The Greek line halted in mid-charge with only fifty feet separating them from the Persians. The Persians fired their weapons as the Greeks dropped to a down position with shields at a forty-five-degree angle.

After the first volley, the Greeks immediately sprang to their feet and continued their charge with spears forward. They were too close for the subsequent lines of Persians to fire their arrows without shooting their own front line in the back. The Persians found themselves about to be engaged by sixteen hundred Greek heavy infantry.

In a few seconds, the Greeks were on the Persians and impaling the archers with the front line of spears. The phalanx held its position; regrouped after their initial charge, re-formed, and then began a slow march forward attacking with low and high spears.

The second rank of archers fired point blank at the Greek phalanx causing few casualties. This second line also fell under the Greek spears; at which time, the third, fourth, and fifth ranks of Persians turned in retreat.

Dien and Senri stopped the advance and began an immediate fast-paced recovery to the narrower part of the Pass. Senri's men withdrew back to the wall and returned back through the Hot Gate as Dien's phalanx re-formed in front of the wagons.

As the archers retreated, a new group of Persians moved forward. This group marched forward in a tight formation similar to a phalanx, and as they got closer, I recognized them as the Immortals. They were following a tactic similar to ours where they would be able to remain in their ranks up to the point of engagement.

When they reached within fifty feet of our phalanx, I told Kron to initiate the helot bowmen by using the flute. This was done.

The helots sprang up from their hiding places in the carts and started shooting random arrows at the approaching Immortals. There were forty bowmen shooting three or four arrows, some of them five or six arrows, every minute. Their success rate of taking down the enemy was awesome. This was largely due to the lack of adequate armor for the Persians.

I smiled, thinking, *We are killing the Persians using Persian arrows.* The Persians were falling in mounds. Entire lines were being taken out at once with each wagon of bowmen firing repeatedly.

I imagined what Dien must be thinking, standing in his phalanx waiting for Xerxes's best troops to attack him without being able to engage. This went on for ten minutes, and the piles of bodies were higher than during the earlier battle. Sometimes, the piles were three or over four men high.

The helot bowmen now began using arrows that had been prepared with oils that would make them torches, once lit. The arrow barrage continued with many of the arrows flaming as they found their targets.

Finally, the Immortals could not advance due to the blocked Pass; and the fact that, they were taking heavy casualties. They began to withdraw and started an organized retreat. As they did, the arrow barrage continued.

It took another three minutes for the last Persian to be out of range of our archers. I am sure this tactic was a surprise to

Xerxes because we are not known for utilizing archers during warfare.

I ordered, by flute, Dien's men to recover from the field and told Kron to go down and move his phalanx forward.

As this was being done, a runner came to give me the report from Illi's phalanx. He reported that Illi's phalanx lost two hundred Arcadians, five Spartans, and Illi. This was a tough pill to swallow after the morning's events. I did not see Illi fall. He went on to report that there were another seventy-five injured. I told the runner that I would appoint a new Spartan captain to lead the phalanx. He left me at that point.

I looked down and saw Kron's phalanx taking the field. I looked behind me and saw Dien's phalanx retiring behind the gate, and I saw Gelon's phalanx moving up to the ready position.

It was not yet noon. I hollered down and told Senri to join me on the wall. I sent a runner to get Gelon to also join me on the wall.

I asked Senri when he arrived how his troops had fared.

He said he lost no Spartans but did lose four other men.

I told him about Illi. Senri took this news hard. He had been close to Illi. We had all been close to Illi.

Gelon climbed the wall.

I told Senri to see to his troops. He was certain to have more action today.

I told Gelon about Illi and asked for his suggestion for a replacement.

He recommended a soldier named Celeas. He said, "Celeas has good tactical experience and is a natural leader."

I told Gelon to go find Celeas, give him the news, and introduce him to Illi's phalanx and the Arcadian leader that goes with them. Gelon left.

I looked down on the battlefield. Without being ordered, the helots and some of Senri's men were clearing away the battlefield once again. I turned to the soldier next to me and told him to alert me if there were any changes. As I came down off the wall, I noticed the wagons were being pulled back through the Hot Gate.

I walked to my tent area with Sari at my side and told him, "I need some nutrition and some rest." I ate a quick meal that Sari had prepared.

I started thinking of what my next maneuver could possibly be that would help preserve more Greek lives. We lost entirely too many men in just a matter of a couple of hours.

While I was in thought, Gelon approached my camp. I bid him, "Sit with me" and offered him nourishment, which he refused.

He advised me that Celeas was now with phalanx one and working with the Arcadians. Gelon said his men were in the ready position behind the wall, and Zee had moved his phalanx up and was resting.

I looked at Gelon and stated, "I do not want to lose any more captains today."

He looked at me and replied, "Neither do I."

I told Gelon to stay out of the front line.

He nodded his acknowledgment.

Then, I did something I seldom do. I asked Gelon, "If you were in my shoes, what would you do next?"

He looked down deep in thought and then rose his eyes up to meet mine and stated, "I would continue to hold the Pass, and try to take advantage of Xerxes's weaknesses."

I thanked him for his candid response.

Gelon said, "I must get back to my men. Then I will man the wall and keep you informed." He hollered over his shoulder as he was leaving, "Get some rest, Leonidas."

I took his advice and went into my tent to lie down. No sooner had I shut my eyes than a runner approached my camp hollering for the king.

Sari intercepted him as well as my now familiar Spartan guard. I exited my tent to find Sari holding a runner at knifepoint and ten Spartans holding spears, at-the-ready. I told them to lower their spears and thanked Sari and asked the runner what his message was.

He said, "Come to the wall immediately."

I thanked him for his message and advised him, "In the future, do not approach my camp hollering, or you may not get to my camp."

He nodded his understanding and left immediately.

I started walking toward the Phocian Wall along with Sari and my Spartan guards. Once I arrived, I noticed Senri's reserves were in formation ready to go through the gate.

I climbed the ladder to the wall and asked Gelon what was going on.

Gelon stated, "The Persians are forming up about a half mile away, and I can see a line of horses behind the spearmen." Without looking at me, he said, "I thought you would want to be informed of this."

I looked into the distance and thanked Gelon. I then knew what was going to happen. The Persians would try to draw us out into the wider portion of the Pass where they could use their cavalry on us. Their cavalry could never operate in our end of the Pass.

I reached my decision. I told a runner to go down, and instruct Senri to have our longest spears passed to Kron's phalanx. I then told the runner to go to Kron, and tell him to advance his phalanx slightly, and explain about the possibility of cavalry.

I said to Gelon, "By advancing the phalanx forty or fifty feet, we would be giving Kron the ability to back-up slowly keeping our men on solid ground."

As I was speaking to Gelon, I observed the helots running out of the gate carrying bundles of our long spears, some of them eight feet, some nine. I looked at Gelon, "With the long spears, they will be able to stop a cavalry attack if necessary."

Gelon nodded his understanding. As we watched the new spears being passed forward, we noticed the enemy was getting closer.

Kron brought his phalanx out of rest with helmets down and shields up and ordered the phalanx to move forward slowly. They moved forward approximately forty to fifty feet, halted, and went to the rest position.

The Persians were now steadily walking forward in their spread-out formation taking up the entire width of the Pass. Kron was still in a narrow area of the Pass and had been instructed not to advance into the wider portion. I waited to see what would occur next.

Once again, the Persians were in lines of men separated by several feet from the next line. As they drew closer, it became evident that the front lines possessed very large battle axes.

These axes would be able to penetrate our armor and our shields.

I sent a runner to find Hemi and bring him to me.

The Persians had closed to within two hundred feet. By now, Kron would have seen the threat. Kron would also realize that he now possessed the exact weapon he needed to counter the battle axes.

Hemi climbed the ladder and approached me. I glanced over my shoulder at him and asked, "Are the bowmen still available and do we have enough arrows for them?"

Hemi smiled and said, "We have thousands of arrows and my bowmen are at your disposal."

I told him, "Gather your bowmen, and get them ready to go out the Hot Gate."

He nodded his understanding and left immediately.

Kron had brought his men to phalanx ready position with low spears forward and high spears forward. In addition, line three of the phalanx also had high spears forward. By using the longer spears, we could increase our threat to the enemy. Kron knew that he could not wait for the Persians to attack because the shields would not withstand their heavy axes. We could not let this occur, or the phalanx would break.

Once again, the Persians congested and became bunched up. The men bearing the battle axes were holding them with both hands due their heavy weight. They had no shields and little armor. The blade of the battle axes appeared to be almost one foot in length. These were huge weapons which I had not seen in the past. The Locrians and Spartans held firm.

When the axmen came to within five feet, Kron's order had the entire phalanx lunge forward with three quick steps while thrusting. The front two lines of axmen fell due to the extreme reach of the longer spears. The Persians assumed that they would strike first against our shields.

The phalanx withdrew three steps. The next group of axmen stumbled over the bodies of the first two lines of axmen. They were now out of their lines.

Kron had the phalanx take three more steps backward. This space gave the axmen time to regroup into their lines as the fourth line crawled over their fallen comrades. Once again, the phalanx faced two new lines of axmen.

Kron ordered the phalanx to rapidly move forward thrusting once again impaling the axmen prior to their attempts to strike with their axes. Two or three of them did get to swing their axes but in mid-stroke were impaled, which took the power out of their swing.

The phalanx was disengaged from the bodies of the axmen and, once again, stepped back. There were now two distinct piles of bodies with spaces between them.

I looked back into the ranks of Persians and noted there were at least ten more lines of axmen. I sent a runner down immediately to instruct Hemi to take his men behind our phalanx and open fire on the enemy with his bowmen.

Spears were being passed up. The process was repeated three more times with very few front-line casualties in the phalanx. The enemy body build-up was becoming extreme.

Hemi and the bowmen started firing randomly. They could not miss. I just hoped they kept the arch of their arrows high enough to avoid the backs of our men in the phalanx. The screams and cries echoed against the wall and rose as the axmen fell, and those behind the axmen started to feel the arrow attack.

I noticed, in the distance, two lines of horsemen just waiting for their opportunity.

The battlefield in front of Kron had over one thousand dead axmen mingled with very few of our own. The arrow barrage from Hemi's bowmen was beginning to have an effect, and the Persian lines were beginning to turn away.

As they did, I could see in the distance men walking and running toward the horsemen. The horses were becoming agitated and rearing up and kicking at soldiers who were trying to escape. Horsemen were being thrown, and a chaotic situation was developing on the Persian side of the field.

I looked down and noticed Kron's men were standing in guard position and the axmen were finally giving up trying to press the attack. Their plan had failed, and we once again held the Pass.

Gelon and I looked at each other and smiled.

The bowmen continued firing until I ordered the flutes to call them off.

Kron brought his phalanx to rest, and they dropped down to one knee. I hollered down to order helots out with water. I sent a runner telling Hemi to withdraw his bowmen.

At this moment, the clouds darkened and the wind came upon us. Our battlefield was already muddy, bloody, and slippery. Rain would just make it worse.

I told the flutes to withdraw Kron's phalanx. I looked down over the wall and called to Senri to move his men away from the gate. He did that instantly. Kron was now marching his phalanx through the gate.

I sent a runner to tell Gelon to wait before he moved onto the field. I wanted to give the helots and our reserves time to clear the field. They were busy disposing of the enemy bodies along with the large axes. Some of the helots were taking the time to recover arrows from the bodies of the Persians.

After the clearing of the battlefield was complete, I ordered Gelon to move his men through the gate to take up his position on the battlefield. He took his phalanx through the gate and brought them to rest.

Kron climbed the ladder and reported that he had lost five Locrians and no Spartans. Kron looked at me and thanked me for sending the large spears out.

I put my arm on his shoulder and said, "I did what you would have done." He smiled and left me.

I was sure, by now, that Xerxes was probably at his extreme level of frustration. He probably wondered what it would take to get us out of our end of the Pass. No matter what he thought of us, he knew one thing for sure; he was up against a trained army, not a bunch of tribesmen. I am sure Xerxes was used to having his enemies surrender upon seeing the site of his huge army, so we posed a dilemma to him.

I imagined, at this point, that the rest of the Spartan Army must certainly be on the move and heading toward our location. The trouble is that it would take over a week for them to get here. I shook my head at these thoughts and kept them to myself.

Senri arrived up on the wall and I asked him to keep his eyes open for me and he agreed.

I left the wall and Sari and I walked back to my camp. I told Sari, "I need to rest."

He nodded acknowledgment, and I went into my tent. I decided to rest with my armor on, just in case.

A short time later, I heard a commotion outside of my tent. Without waiting for Sari, I exited my tent to find my Spartan guard holding an enemy soldier, one of the axmen, who had been wounded but not killed. He was bleeding but did not appear to have life-threatening injuries.

Normally, when the phalanx moves forward, the sharpened spear-butts from the men usually dispenses with any survivors. However, our tactic today did not have us advancing over the bodies, so any wounded were not killed by our men.

The Persian was questioned by my Spartan guard, and Senri had ordered him to be brought to me.

I looked at the Persian and said, "I will not kill you. We will even care for your wounds, but you will be a prisoner. What can you divulge to us about what is going on in your camp?"

The Persian asked for water.

I instructed the Spartans to seat the Persian at my camp and provide him water. I also instructed the Spartan guard to go seek out a surgeon to assist our prisoner. The Persian seemed shocked with the care we were willing to give him. I could see and sense that he was an unwilling warrior.

After drinking, he looked up at me and asked, "You are the King?"

I nodded, stating, "I am the king of the Spartans, and I am acting as the commander of the Greek forces." He accepted this information.

I asked, "What of your camp?"

He said, "Xerxes is killing people for their failure to take the Pass. Many of the troops are afraid to attack because you have defended the Pass regardless of our tactics. We look at it as a death sentence to be ordered to attack you. If we fail, we face death from Xerxes. Our hearts are not in this battle.

There is only fear in our camp. Xerxes is trying to find the path your men took to attack his camp from behind. He killed your Spartans and tortured some trying to get them to tell the way to get behind you. None of them spoke."

I told the prisoner, "We will care for you, but you are still a prisoner. We may have a use for you further."

He nodded his understanding.

At that moment, a surgeon arrived, and I instructed him to care for the prisoner. The prisoner was taken away under Spartan guard but would be looked after by our surgeon.

It was now mid-afternoon, and the day was going fairly well. I could think of no more tricks to deceive the enemy and decided to stay at our end of the Pass. I am sure Xerxes is at his wit's end. I reflected on what the prisoner had told us about Xerxes killing his own men when they failed in their attempts to take the Pass.

Since rest was impossible, I decided that I would call a quick meeting of the leaders and my captains.

Before I could do this, a runner came from Senri telling me that the Persians were forming again. I acknowledged the message and thanked the runner. Before I could ask, Sari was at my side with my equipment, and we began walking to the wall.

Before I could get to the wall, I could hear sounds of conflict on the outside. I scrambled up the wall to witness Gelon's phalanx fully engaged with Persian cavalry. Even though we were in a narrow end of the Pass, the cavalry had made a decision to charge us with the idea of running through our phalanx and breaking us that way.

The scene I looked down on was horrific. The first line of cavalry had run into our spearmen and shields, but the force of the weight of the horses had penetrated into our phalanx. This occurred because of the push from the back lines of the horses that were congested into the small area of the Pass. Some of our men and some horsemen had fallen off the cliff. Some horses were lying down obviously impaled by spears, and at this moment, the phalanx was somewhat disarrayed.

I could see Gelon trying to reorganize the phalanx and direct his men. I now wished we had kept the large spears on the field. Some of Gelon's men had been knocked over by horses creating deep cuts in the phalanx. On top of that, some of the mounted cavalry were throwing javelins from horseback creating further holes in our phalanx.

I told Senri to take his reserves to the field immediately. I further instructed him to take the long spears with him. I also realized, as Senri left, that this would take a few minutes. My hope was that Gelon could hold out until the reserves arrived.

I left the wall momentarily to go down to talk to Senri. I told Senri, that once he got to the field; take his men to the left flank. "Remain in a ten-across formation; march straight ahead with your spears forward until you have extended beyond this battle, stop your phalanx, turn to the sea, use the triple-spear formation and march forward driving everything toward the cliff. If you do not kill it, or if it does not get out of your way, it goes over the cliff; man, beast, whatever. Go now!"

I quickly went back up the ladder to notice that Gelon had backed up somewhat with his troops to regain his formation. I could also see many of our troops on the ground.

I fluted down the information to Gelon that the reserves were coming in. He immediately closed his formation as tight as possible with spears forward.

Horsemen were still trying to attack the phalanx but having much more trouble with the footing and the inability to push forward.

At this moment, Senri's men came in behind Gelon's phalanx and took over the left flank. They squeezed by Gelon's men. With spears forward, they began a quick-time advance onto the left side of the battlefield. They met little resistance having momentum against the mostly stationary cavalry.

Once they achieved the distance they needed, they stopped abruptly turning the phalanx toward the sea. They were now eighty across and ten deep. At this time, Gelon's phalanx was at one end of the Pass forty wide, but no longer twenty deep due to our losses.

Once Senri's phalanx was aimed in the direction of the sea, and as if on cue, both phalanxes began moving forward. As the horsemen tried to attack Senri's phalanx, they were met with long spears that were able to impale both horse and rider before they could contact his men. Most of the javelins had been thrown by the horsemen, and they had begun using their long swords which had no effect on the phalanx due to the large Greek shields. The horsemen were being squeezed and turned into a smaller area, many starting to slip over the cliff, others beginning to retreat.

The far left flank of Senri's phalanx appeared to be exposed; however, the men on the far left were walking at a side angle keeping their spears in the direction of the West Gate. This deterred any counter-attacking on our left flank.

Both phalanxes were moving at a rapid pace having to step over horses and riders who had been impaled by our long spears. This was a horrific sight from my vantage point; but once again, the Greek phalanx was doing its job in taking the field.

As the two phalanxes closed together, a portion of the left flank of Senri's phalanx was able to turn toward the West Gate to protect the area between the mountainside and the back of his phalanx.

Once the gap between the two phalanxes was closed and the killing completed in that area, the two phalanxes were both turned to the West. We were covering the entire Pass with approximately 160 across and 10 deep in some places. As I watched this, I realized all the training of all the years had come to fruition for these fine soldiers. I further realized, had it not been for Gelon and Senri possessing the leadership qualities to handle these tactics, we would have taken far more casualties during this battle. I noticed in the distance that the horsemen were retreating.

Zee appeared beside me on the wall telling me he had brought his men up.

I told him that we had taken some heavy losses from Gelon's phalanx. I instructed him to take the field with his men and relieve Gelon. "Stay out in the field next to Senri's reserves. Take the long spears, you may need them."

Zee nodded and left immediately.

The battlefield looked horrendous as Gelon brought his men to one knee in rest position. Senri followed suit and brought his men to one knee.

Zee re-equipped his men with long spears and then marched his men through the gate. They marched forward stepping over horses and dead including our own. This is hard to do but must be done.

After they moved forward, they moved over to the left flank and I told the flutes to recall Gelon. Gelon brought his men to their feet and ordered them to about-face. He then marched his men back toward the gate.

Once Gelon's men left the field, Zee brought his men up to the right flank to take the position vacated by Gelon. Zee brought his men to rest.

I could see in the distance the Persians were not through. They were mounting yet another attack with another group of soldiers. I could not yet see what they were carrying, but I felt it was wise for us to have our long spears on the field.

Gelon's men recovered through the Hot Gate and went to the rear of our area to rest.

I sent a runner down to order the helots to clear the field. I knew it would take some time to remove the many horses as well as the many bodies. The helots went to the field immediately and went to work.

As I looked down, it was a depressing battlefield, and I knew we could not afford such losses and continue to fight here. I braced myself, for I was sure I would hear about this later from the other coalition leaders.

I noticed behind me that Celeas had brought up phalanx one to the ready position. I sent a runner down to bring Celeas up to me.

The clearing of the battlefield was going slowly, and I was concerned because Persian troops were already advancing and had closed to within one-half of a mile.

We were now positioned well beyond our normal battle area, but this was only due to what had just transpired.

Celeas joined me on the wall. I asked Celeas if he was ready.

He said he was.

I told him that Gelon's phalanx had taken heavy losses, and I had not yet heard the numbers. "The men on the field right now are using our long spears. We do not have enough long spears to completely outfit your phalanx."

He nodded his understanding.

I told him to stay with me on the wall. We spoke no further.

The helots were making good progress now and had recovered our injured and dead.

Gelon appeared beside me on the wall looking very exhausted. I asked if he had a report yet. He said, "It is incomplete, but we have lost over two hundred men, most of them Corinthians and Arcadians, but we did lose some Spartans as well."

Gelon went on to explain, "When the cavalrymen began throwing their javelins, the Corinthians and Arcadians were not prepared for this tactic; therefore, they suffered great losses. We did lose seven Spartans."

I told Gelon to go rest and see to his men.

I looked at Celeas and said, "You man the wall for a while. I am going to my tent."

As I said this, I looked out over the field to see the Persians running in a full charge toward our lines. I said to Celeas, "I think I will stay for a while."

I noticed Dien had brought his phalanx up behind Celeas's group, and Dien was making his way toward the wall.

At that moment, the first attackers were running into our phalanx and bouncing off, as usual. The phalanx did not have spears forward as they were waiting for more of the enemy to arrive. The battle was happening a little farther out, and it was harder to see the details.

It appeared that Zee and Senri had things in hand, but I was disturbed that our reserves were now involved in their third engagement for the day.

As more and more Persians arrived, I observed the phalanx disengage and go to spears forward. They then began an organized thrusting attack spanning the entire two-phalanx formation. I could hear the screams of the enemy falling as the methodically coordinated attack continued.

It was, as if, the Persians had learned nothing in two days of warfare with us. We had probably killed over ten thousand of their men to hundreds of our own.

Senri and Zee were working together taking steps forward slowly, attacking, then slowly stepping back to attain footing on the battlefield that was now littered with the dead.

I noticed that they were slowly withdrawing back into the narrower portion of the Pass. In a matter of minutes, Senri's men were at the back of the formation, and Zee's men were back in our normal defensive area.

The attack from the enemy was in no way organized. It was random and was very suicidal from my observation point.

I told the flute to recall Senri. This was done, and Senri's men marched back through the Hot Gate. I sent a runner to get Senri.

I looked beside me to find Dien standing there observing the battle.

Senri came up the ladder, and I addressed him. "See to your men's rest."

I looked at Dien. "Until the reserves are rested, your phalanx will go out if needed."

I told Celeas to go down with his men, and leave me a position in the second line. Celeas and Dien both left the wall.

The enemy soldiers were still trying to attack Zee's phalanx but were having no success against the long spears. The dead were piling up, and Zee would step back accordingly. The enemy would climb over the dead troops only to meet the spears of the Spartans and add to the pile of dead. This kept going for a period of time to the point where Zee's men were backed up against the Phocian Wall. They could no longer move backward.

The enemy was losing men in the hundreds and thousands, but they were relentless. I, once again, sent for Hemi.

Hemi was at the bottom of the wall anticipating our need of his services, once again. He scrambled up the ladder, and I asked him if his bowmen could serve us yet again.

He asked what I wanted him to do.

I told him that our tactics had brought the enemy very close to the Phocian Wall. I asked if his bowmen could fire into the enemy lines from the Phocian Wall. He said he would do this immediately.

He left the wall, and I looked down at Zee's situation. There was nowhere else to back up. The enemy probably thought they were breaking us because they were so close to our wall.

Behind me, the archers started to arrive. I told the archers that there were plenty of targets and to shoot into the distance as much as possible to slow the masses down that were pressing against our phalanx.

The forty archers began shooting immediately. Arrows were being passed up by their fellow helots, and once again, we were using Xerxes's weapons against him. These bowmen were very accurate.

I was impressed with their skills. I decided, then and there, that if I survived this event, things were going to change. The helots had played an important role in this war, and that was not going to be forgotten. The helots were raining arrows down as fast as they could reload. This was having an effect on the attacking Persians.

Finally, the Persians turned from the attack and started leaving our end of the Pass. As this occurred, their front-most troops were unable to retreat and were slowly picked off by our bowmen.

Zee's men were very pressed together, and I called with the flutes for them to recover behind the wall.

The helots and some of Dien's men, who were acting as reserves, sprang into action once again to try to clear the battlefield.

It did not appear that Zee had taken many casualties. I still waited to hear the results from Gelon.

I somehow know that even though it is late in the afternoon, the Persians are not done. I sent word, by runner, for Celeas to hold his position until the field is cleared.

The thought occurred to me, *We have to do all the work of clearing the field because all the killing is occurring on our end of the field.*

Zee recovered his troops taking them to rest.

It took the helots and one hundred of the reserves to clear the field that was now red mush. It was hard to look at, but if there was ever any ground that had been fought over, this small area would be at the top. It took thirty minutes for the field to be cleared in our normal battle area.

I used the flute to order Celeas's men to move forward. Phalanx two, with Dien, moved up to the ready position. I noticed Kron moving his phalanx up behind Dien.

Gelon joined me on the wall and reported that 150 Arcadians had been killed, 95 Corinthians, 7 Spartans, and another 100 injured. I shook my head at these losses. We had lost over 500 men today, and the day was not over.

I told Gelon to go back to his troops and on his way, send Senri up. I did not think that it was over for today.

I wondered, *How many more men were going to die today at the hand of Xerxes because they failed their king?*

Senri joined me on the wall. I told him, "You will have to replenish the phalanxes with your reserves. This will cut you down considerably. See to it as soon as you can so the men can become familiar with their new groups."

Senri acknowledged this and left.

The field was cleared, and Celeas marched phalanx one out to our normal position. Celeas brought his men to rest, relieving one Spartan, providing a space for me.

Dien then joined me on the wall as his men moved up to the ready position.

Kron had moved up behind him.

I asked Dien to stay on the wall for me, and if he should have to go into battle with his men, get Kron to relieve him. I told him, "I am going to have a quick meeting with the leaders and other captains at my tent area. If anything important comes of this meeting, I will personally inform you."

Dien said that he would watch the wall.

I left the wall and walked back to my camp with Sari. I asked Sari to summon the other leaders and the rest of the captains. Sari went to do this immediately.

I left my armor on and sat by my tent. After a short time, the leaders started to trickle in, and I bid them, "Sit with me." Except for Dien and Celeas, my captains also arrived.

I looked over the faces and could sense what some of these leaders were thinking. I knew they were not soldiers, but they were leaders. I was making them soldiers. I looked at the Arcadian leader. Out of the two groups of Arcadians who had arrived, one of their leaders was now dead. In two days of fighting, the Arcadians had lost over one-fourth of the fighting force they had sent to help us, over four hundred men. The Corinthians had also lost many today. Yesterday, the Locrians had heavy losses.

I looked at the remaining Arcadian leader and said, "I am sorry for the heavy losses your troops have endured. We are sending you Arcadians from the reserves to help fill the ranks back to one hundred percent. We are also sending reserves from Tegea and Malis to fill the ranks of the Corinthians."

I looked over the group and said, "Your men fought bravely today and handled themselves well in the phalanx. We were surprised, but we have taken the day so far."

The Corinthian leader asked, "How long do you think we can do this, Leonidas?"

I looked at him and said, "As long as it takes."

He said, "When will the rest of the Spartans arrive? When will we be relieved?"

I told him, "I have not received word, but I am sure the Spartan Army is only days away." This comment set well with the leaders, and they accepted the fact that we would stay until relieved.

I could not say this to their faces, but I was thinking, *If the various city-states had sent more men, to begin with, maybe we would not be under such duress.* I held my tongue on this thought remembering that I was holding together a very fragile coalition.

I told them, "At this moment, phalanx one is on the field holding a position for me. Phalanx two is acting as reserves for the moment, and phalanx three is ready behind them."

I further advised them, "The reserves have fought three times today and are in serious need of rest. Also, we have depleted our reserves in order to refill your phalanxes to full strength."

The Locrian leader asked, "Why don't we just make all of our phalanxes larger and not have the reserves?"

I looked at him and said, "The reserves are what have allowed your group to only need to fight one time today. Also, there is no point in making the phalanx any larger due to the confined area we are operating in." I did acknowledge that the Locrian had a fair question, but for the moment, our reserves provided a very important function.

I looked at the men and told them to get as much rest as they could. See that their men are fed; and hopefully, this day will end without any more Greek deaths. I dismissed the leaders and told Sari that I would dine.

I was left alone with my thoughts constantly questioning if I said the right thing or pushed too far. When I became a Spartan king, I did not know that I would be directing and managing other leaders and their troops.

I dined and told Sari, once again, "Please join me for my meal."

As I sat eating my meal, I was once again disturbed by a runner approaching from the wall. He advised me that Captain Dien was requesting that I come to the wall. I dropped my plate and told Sari to bring my armor. I accompanied the runner back to the wall followed by ten Spartans.

When I arrived at the wall, Dien was waiting for me. We climbed up on top. He advised me that the Persians were apparently preparing for another attack. The Persians were approximately one mile away and closing. At this moment, Kron joined us on the wall. The three of us stood there straining our eyes to the distance trying to see what was coming next.

I told Kron that he would only go out on the field again if Dien's men needed to take the field in reserve. I instructed Kron to stay on the wall, and Dien and I left the wall.

At the bottom of the ladder, Sari was waiting with my helmet, shield, and spear.

On the way through the Hot Gate, I told Dien to send a runner for Gelon to bring his phalanx up behind Kron. I then told Dien that I was going out onto the field to join my phalanx alongside Celeas.

I walked out onto the field for the second time today leaving my Spartan bodyguard behind. When I arrived at the phalanx, I took up my position in the space Celeas had provided for me.

I then left my position and went out in front of the phalanx and addressed them. It was easy to be heard with the wall of rock rising up on one side and the wall behind us. I addressed the Arcadians and Spartans as *Greeks*. I told the Arcadians that they had lost many of their citizens today, but they had held. Hopefully, we would be the last group to fight today.

The Arcadians appeared to me to have grown up today. They were all seasoned veterans having been through battle earlier in the day.

Before I could say another word, the Arcadians and Spartans came to attention and offered me a salute. I was taken aback by this. I returned the salute with my own spear and retook up my position in the phalanx.

My mind was racing wondering what our phalanx would face next from the Persians. I remembered that the Persians prefer to use archers and cavalry when possible to weaken their enemies. It had not worked earlier, but I wondered if Xerxes would try to catch us off guard with archers.

The troops that were approaching us were now approximately one-half of a mile away. I went back out in front of the phalanx and told the men, "I have no evidence to support my theory, but be on the alert for the down command in the event of archers. Don't be surprised if horsemen once again charge us, especially if we are in the down position. I want you to be prepared."

I got back into the phalanx and ordered the man next to me to go to the Hot Gate. "Order the helots to bring up the long spears and have them passed up to the front ranks. These spears will be set down beside us. We will have them ready in the event of a cavalry charge."

I could think of nothing else to do other than stay within the phalanx and trust our tactics. The runner returned two minutes later advising me that it was being done.

I looked behind me and saw that Kron was on the wall, knowing fully, he would alert us if he saw something coming that we did not anticipate. I brought the men out of rest position and came to the phalanx-ready position. We waited.

The Persians were approaching in their typical spread-out lines, which meant, they would congest as they got closer to us. From our position, I could not detect archers or cavalry.

The men facing us were colorfully dressed having red scarves and bluish-colored headdresses. They were carrying spears and the traditional small wicker shields. They were one hundred feet away, and the front lines began to congest as they approached our position.

I brought my phalanx to spears forward and we waited. As the enemy continued to approach, I ordered, "Phalanx, FORWARD." I wanted to give us plenty of room to back up due to the pile-up of bodies.

As the front lines of the Persians closed, they broke ranks sprinting toward our position. Instead of hearing the sound of the approaching enemy hitting our shields, I heard their screams as they were impaled on our spears.

I ordered the phalanx to its tightest formation, instantly feeling the pressure of the shield behind me on my back. We were now like a tightly coiled spring impaling the enemy as they arrived. The full width of our phalanx was now engaged and appeared to be handling the enemy easily.

As with the past battles, the bodies started to pile up making it even harder for the enemy's spears to reach our men. I ordered the phalanx to step back three steps and hold. This allowed the front lines of the Persians to climb over the dead and continue their attack.

In the midst of this, my attention was drawn overhead as I saw a volley of arrows descending on us. Before the order could be given, arrows were penetrating the phalanx. The helmets we wore prevented much damage; however, the shock of an arrow attack coming in the midst of an engagement surprised us. There were so many lines of spearmen that I could not tell where the arrows were coming from.

I did notice some of the arrows were killing their own men. The archers would be guessing at our location and were assuming we would remain stationary.

I passed the order left and right to advance the phalanx. This was done, and we started the slow methodical forward movement of the killing machine. As we stepped over the dead, our front two lines continued engaging the enemy with spear-thrusts. As we walked over the bodies, the remaining lines of the phalanx finished any survivors with their sharp spear-butts.

We kept moving forward, and the arrows kept coming. The lines behind me were trying to raise their shields slightly, but the phalanx insisted on them keeping their shields in the back of the person in front of them. The phalanx, beyond the third line, was walking forward with their heads as low as possible, almost crouching, but still pushing the phalanx forward.

After another fifty feet, we had lost some of our men from the arrow attack, and the Pass was beginning to widen. I ordered the phalanx to gradually expand.

We kept moving forward and killing as we went. There was nothing we could do about the archers. We did not even know where they were. They had apparently been told we were moving forward, because their arrows were now having a greater effect of shooting their own men in the back, just making our job easier. It was a chaotic scene being barraged by arrows bouncing off our armor and shields as enemy troops fell in front of us and underneath our spears and feet. The screams of men were everywhere, but the phalanx held firm.

We got to the extended position on the field where we were eighty across and ten deep in some places. We had taken some casualties, but the phalanx was still holding. I brought the phalanx to a halt. I knew that if we moved farther into the Pass, we could be easily flanked. Also, I did not know if there was cavalry waiting for us to move farther into the Pass.

I heard flutes behind me and observed over my shoulder that Dien's troops were taking the field to support us.

I looked back around in time to see the man in front of me fall from a spear-thrust. I went to the front line taking his position.

Celeas did not like this, hollering for me to be replaced.

I hollered back, "Hold your position!"

I then ordered the phalanx to advance at a rapid rate. The phalanx started moving eighty across at a rapid pace killing men, knocking others over who were trampled underfoot. It was very hard to maintain footing while walking across bodies at a rapid pace, and the bodies were falling as fast as we were moving.

Once again, this tactic created confusion in the Persian lines. Men realized they were about to be trampled or stabbed and were trying to turn and retreat.

The arrows were still coming but not as many. I could not count how many lines of enemy spearmen we had overrun, but we were now getting into a much wider area of the Pass.

About this time, I noticed Dien's phalanx rapidly coming up on our left. He brought his phalanx up at forty wide and then spread some of his men into my phalanx to replace our losses.

We were well away from the wall now, but I still heard the flute call that meant more troops were taking the field. That meant Kron was bringing his men up and out onto the field. I wondered what my captains were doing but turned my attention back to the enemy who was now trying to retreat instead of face our spears.

The increased phalanx, numbering approximately 120 men across and 10 deep, kept advancing into the Persian lines at a very rapid rate. I now saw lines of archers who had been hiding behind 40 or 50 lines of spearmen.

We were now exposed on our left to being flanked. We had come out into the Pass very far. The going was easier because we were now chasing the enemy and killing them as they tried to escape. They were running into each other in their attempts to avoid our spears. As they did this, it disrupted the lines of archers putting a halt to the arrow attack.

I then noticed Kron's phalanx appear on the left and joined up with Dien's providing a new left flank. We were now 160 across and 10 deep with the exception of Kron's phalanx which was 20 deep.

My phalanx was tiring, but I felt like we needed to finish the day strong, so I ordered the men to slow the advance, and continue at a reduced pace. As we moved farther into the Pass, Kron widened our phalanx to include two hundred across. Looking down to the left, it was a beautiful sight to see the three phalanxes advancing without any interruption in our step as the enemy had now broken out of their ranks and were in full retreat.

I decided at that moment, if horsemen came, we would encircle them with our three phalanxes. But, my phalanx was tired; I called a halt and the other two phalanxes halted as well. The Greek fighting force had become a precision machine.

I called for the withdrawal of my troops first. My phalanx backed up, turned to about-face, and made a rapid withdrawal back to the narrow end near the wall.

As we did this, Dien's men, who had filled out our phalanx, returned back to his phalanx once we withdrew. Dien's and Kron's phalanxes were now covering an area 160 men across.

Once my men recovered to their original position, I ordered them to withdraw back through the Hot Gate.

I told Celeas to take command and take his men to camp for rest.

I then turned to look over the battlefield. I was standing among more dead men than I had seen in my entire life at one particular battle.

Dien's men were now recovering as I had done. They re-formed to forty across leaving room for Kron to withdraw his men. Kron's men continued to withdraw through the Hot Gate. Once this maneuver was complete, Dien's men took up the guard position in front of the wall. He then brought his men to rest.

At this moment, I left the field. I thought over what had occurred. We had been subject to an arrow attack while the enemy was engaging us. This meant that the prisoner we had questioned was being truthful. Xerxes continued to demonstrate his willingness to kill his own men.

I arrived through the Hot Gate and handed my helmet, spear, and shield to Sari.

I immediately climbed the ladder to the wall. I looked behind me and Gelon's men were in the ready position.

Kron's men were at the gate in reserve position. Kron then joined me on the wall as well as Gelon. I looked at the both of them and stated, "Xerxes has to be a madman to shoot his own men in an attempt to shoot us."

I knew without asking, Celeas would send a runner with a report of his dead and wounded. My hope now was that the last battle of the day had now occurred.

I asked Kron why he took the field.

He said, "It appeared that you would need a wider phalanx, and from my observation position, it looked as though you took a substantial number of casualties in your phalanx. This was made clear to me by observing that Dien had sent some of his men over to fill out your phalanx." He looked me in the eye and said, "I did what I thought you would have done."

I thanked him. I told him to go see to his men.

I asked Gelon to watch the wall for me. I left the wall and told Sari I would try to rest.

As we were leaving the wall area, I noticed the helots and some of Kron's men were taking the field to clear their dead and recover our wounded and dead.

I told Sari, "Leave me to me rest unless it is very important. I will meet with the leaders once we are assured that no further attacks will occur today."

Sari nodded his understanding.

I took my full armor off hoping it would not be needed again today. I realized my exhaustion and tried to sleep.

I was awakened and noticed it was dark. Sari was gentle and told me the leaders and my captains were waiting around my fire.

I thanked him for letting me rest.

I also received his report from Celeas that fifty-two Arcadians had died largely due to the arrows, and Celeas also lost five Spartans. Dien reported losing three Spartans and twelve perioikoi. Kron reported losing three Locrians.

I thanked Sari for this news and went out to greet the leaders. I told them, "We have taken the day again, but have had heavy losses, especially from the Arcadians."

I looked at the Arcadian leader and told him, "Your sacrifice will not be forgotten."

We had lost over six hundred men today, but I noted that in the last battle alone, we probably killed six thousand men. I said to the leaders, "I too have lost many men. Out of the three hundred Spartans I brought here, over fifty are gone."

The Locrian leader asked, "What of tomorrow?"

The Corinthian leader said, "We cannot last if we continue to take these losses."

I looked down and thought for a moment. I decided to be totally honest in my feelings.

I looked around the campfire with all eyes on me. I said:

You have come here as I have in defense of Greece. Arcadia, the Spartans, the perioikoi, and many others did not need to come this far north to defend our home territories. We came to defend Greece. You, and all of your men, and I and my small group of men, are doing what we agreed to do.

Yet, Sparta is who you wait on as your relief. We are not waiting for any other group of soldiers from any of your city-states. We are waiting on the Spartans. The Spartans will arrive in time. We are being defended from the sea largely by Athenian ships; that is their contribution. I am sure all of your cities feel that they gave what they should, but at the end of the day; who is it you wait on? Whose captains and troops have fought in every phalanx, and what will you do tomorrow? The answers you want from me, I cannot give. I can only tell you, the Spartans will stay here and fight to the last.

I will entertain any suggestions or ideas you have on how to better defend the Pass, but keep in mind, the Spartan phalanx has helped keep more of your men alive than if we had not utilized and shared this information with you.

I told you before, you are my brothers. I do not take it lightly when any of our troops fall. We are facing a barbarian and a tyrant who does not mind killing his own men to achieve his victory. The Spartan phalanx has prevented his victory so far. Tomorrow, we will once again get into our phalanx and march to the battlefield and defend Greece. Go see to your men, for tomorrow will certainly be a trial.

Remember this; there are two walls out there. One is known as the *Phocian Wall;* the other is the *Greek Wall.* The Greek Wall is what we present to Xerxes. It represents us and all of our unity. We are the Greek Wall!

At this moment, the leaders nodded their understanding and started leaving to return to their camps.

I held my captains back. Dien's men had been relieved by Senri's reserves who were now on the wall. A contingent of Spartans and other city-states were out in front of the wall. The rest of his men were now resting behind the wall.

Kron stated that his phalanx would begin the next day as he was only on the field for a short time.

I agreed that this was a good plan. So, it was agreed upon: day three would be led by Kron, then Gelon, then Zee. After that, we would start with Celeas and phalanx one.

I asked my captains if they had any suggestions of how to better defend the Pass without taking such heavy losses.

None of them spoke.

I thanked them for helping me today and told them that I appreciate them more than they can understand. "Go get rest, but wake me if something occurs in the night."

I told Sari to bring me some food and to join me. He did this without speaking, and we ate together in silence.

I realized, once again, how important our helot servants had been to us with their bowmen and javelin throwers. While assisting us with battle, they still are able to serve their Spartan soldiers in the same way Sari serves me.

After dining, I walked to the wall, climbed the ladder, noticing my guard of men trailing behind me. Once I got up on the wall, I found Senri there. Senri appeared very alert and rested, and I was happy to see this.

I told Senri that he had done a good job, and his reserves had fought well today. I also told him, "Dom would be proud of you." I instructed him to alert me if there was any activity.

Senri said, "Maybe when you wake up, the Persians will have left."

I smiled at this attempted humor and bid Senri, "Good night."

I returned to my camp and told Sari, "Wake me before dawn."

The camp became quiet, and the smell of campfires and sea air helped mask the stench of battle.

Our helots had cleared the field once again as best as they could.

I knew that this could be my last night of sleep. I did let my mind wander of what I could have done differently. I, also, was beginning to feel some guilt for bringing so many men into a battle that I could not conceive of how we could ever win. Yet, to this point, we had persevered. But, out of the men we had brought here, one thousand were now dead.

And what of the Phocians; how are they faring? Are they following their agreement to guard our rear? All these questions and thoughts seem to be without answers.

I reflected upon the battles of the day. The fighting today had been far more intense than of the previous day. Both sides had greater losses. I sensed that whatever Xerxes was telling his generals, the intensity level had definitely been extreme today. I can't imagine a worse day or more difficult day than we had just encountered.

I fell to sleep out of exhaustion.

CHAPTER TWELVE

THE LAST PHALANX

Ninth Day at Thermopylae

*A dark cloud comes down the mountain into the Pass.
It meets a dark cloud from the other end of the Pass,
but in the middle of the two clouds shines a light. The
day will be lost, but the light will shine on.*

I was awakened rudely by Sari calling me. "You must come quickly."

I immediately left my tent to find Spartans holding a male prisoner and asked, "What is going on?"

The Spartan guard, Gallus, stated: "Our forward positions encountered eighteen men from the enemy camp wishing to escape. These men were unarmed and had passed by Xerxes's watch. This one, in particular, asked to speak with you to offer information."

I looked at the man and asked what he had to say.

He said, "I am Theus and I am Greek. We were forced to fight in Xerxes's army after surrendering our small village. I have important information for you."

I looked at him and waited.

He said, "Xerxes, with the help of a Greek, has found the path that leads over the mountain and down to Alpeni. During the day, he has sent thousands of troops and archers onto the path."

I looked at the man with great concern. I asked, "Exactly how many thousands?"

He said, "Many thousands."

I looked at him and the guards and said, "Free this man and the others."

I then turned to Gallus and told him, "Summon the leaders." It was now about four in the morning.

I told Sari, "Buildup the campfire for my meeting." I sat by the fire and waited for my captains and the leaders to join me. As I waited, I determined that we would not have time to send help to the Phocians.

I told Sari, "Bring me a reliable runner who can get a message to the Phocians."

As I did this, the Greek who had just provided me with information returned. He faced me and stated, "I was wrong about the time that Xerxes sent troops onto the path. The time I provided you referred to the last group of Persians who entered the path. Many more soldiers had already gone before them. I cannot tell you the exact time when the first soldiers went on the path."

I thanked the Greek and he left.

Knowing that the path is narrow, I realized that the Persians could have been sending troops up the path all day long. This meant they could be arriving at our defensive position any time now. I decided that I should still send a runner. I knew that it would take several hours for a runner to get to where the Phocians had taken up position.

While in thought, the captains and the leaders drifted into my camp. I bid them, "Sit," as did I.

I told them of the information from the escaped Greek. I could see the stunned shock in the eyes of the leaders. "We can only guess when the Persians might engage the Phocians. I do not feel comfortable sending reinforcements to the Phocians."

I further advised the leaders of my plan to send a runner to alert the Phocians, but I explained, "My real feeling is that the Phocians will already be engaged before he arrives. If the Greek is correct, the Phocians will not be able to stand against the Persians."

The leaders looked at me waiting for my orders. I said, "We will abandon Thermopylae. I instruct each of you to take your men, and leave Thermopylae as quickly as possible."

Then I said, "The Spartans will stay." This statement stunned the leaders.

The Arcadian leader said, "It would be suicidal to stay with your remaining 250 men."

I looked at him and said, "Somebody has to keep Xerxes and his men busy to allow you to escape."

The Thespian leader stood and stated, "The Thespians will stand with the Spartans."

The leader from Thebes also stood and stated, "We, as well, will stand with the Spartans."

I could not argue with the offer that they presented, but I did state, "The rest of you must escape and meet up with the

Spartan force that is on its way to Thermopylae." I ended the meeting by telling the leaders to follow my orders.

I told the leader of Thebes and the leader of the Thespians, "We will meet soon to discuss our tactics." Both leaders nodded their understanding and the meeting dispersed.

I held my captains and advised them, "Tell the Spartans to release their helot servants and order them to go home."

Sari was at the fringe of our meeting and immediately interjected, "No Master, you cannot send us away. We are proud servants of the Spartans and cannot be dismissed as unimportant."

After hearing this, I turned my attention back to the captains. I said, "I would prefer that the helots go home. It will be your decision and each Spartan's decision what will become of his individual servant. However, I do order all the supply assistants, cooks, and additional support helpers to go home immediately." I broke this meeting up telling my captains, "I will consider our strategy and meet with you soon."

I turned to Sari who had brought me a runner. I asked the runner, "Do you know of the mountain path that comes around behind us and into Alpeni?"

He said, "I am aware of it."

I told him to go to the Phocians and advise them that they are about to be attacked. "The force that will attack them will be large. Tell them that no reinforcements will be coming. Thermopylae is going to be abandoned. If the Phocians are already engaged, come back immediately."

As I was giving the helot instructions, Gelon interrupted me. He told the helot to wait and asked for a private counsel with me. We walked away from all who could hear us.

Gelon said, "Leonidas, I have a Spartan soldier who is a distance runner. Please allow him to go instead of the helot. His conditioning may take many minutes off the journey. Also, he will be able to provide exact military information to the Phocians. His reports, after returning, will be more accurate as well."

I thought for a moment and then agreed with his idea. We walked back and dismissed the helot.

I instructed Gelon, "Send your man immediately."

I told Sari, "Wake up the reader, and bring me the sacrifice."

The two groups who had volunteered to stay had taken minimal losses over the last two days. Between them and the Spartans, we numbered over twelve hundred men. I knew that once the Phocians broke, there would be many thousands of men behind us and we would be totally cut off.

When Sari returned with the reader, I instructed him, "Send a runner to the port, and advise the navy that we are abandoning Thermopylae with the exception of twelve hundred men."

I took the sacrifice and went off by myself slowly, realizing that this is the last animal that would die so that I might receive the *reading-of-the-day*.

I killed the bird and opened it up. I handed the bird to the reader and waited. Megis took his time realizing the importance of this event.

Megis came back to me, faced me and said, "A dark cloud comes down the mountain into the Pass. It meets a dark cloud from the other end of the Pass, but in the middle of the two clouds shines a light. The day will be lost, but the light will shine on."

I looked at the reader and told him that I accepted his reading.

The camp, in darkness, was loud with the movement of troops gathering their equipment and setting about to leave Thermopylae.

Sari returned reporting that the navy was being informed of our situation. I then asked Sari to summon the Theban and Thespian leaders as well as my captains.

I waited by my camp in silence. When the captains and the leaders arrived, I was advised that the rest of the troops would be pulled out within the hour as well as all the support people and supply wagons.

I told them, "We need to hold the Pass as long as possible. This will allow more time for the group who is escaping to get to safe ground."

I further advised that I had sent a runner to inform the navy of our position. I also stated, "I feel that the Phocians are probably already engaged only giving us a little over three hours before we will be flanked."

I studied the leaders' faces for a moment and then I spoke. "The Thespians and the Spartans will face the Persians as we have been doing on our normal field of battle. The Thebans, along with two-hundred Thespians, will defend the East Gate. This disbursement will allow us to have approximately six hundred men in each phalanx." I looked at the Theban leader stating, "You will command the phalanx at the East Gate."

The Thespian leader asked, "How many Spartans do you have left?"

I advised him that there were two hundred and forty-two.

As I was meeting with the leaders, Sari walked up and said that he and several other helots would like to stay and fight with us.

I looked at him and said, "You need to go back to Sparta."

I looked at my men and the leaders, and then I looked back at Sari and said, "We need people we can trust to go back and tell the story of what occurred here."

Sari just stood motionless with a group of thirty-eight helots behind him. I looked at Senri and said, "When this meeting is over, provide these men with some armor."

Senri nodded his understanding.

I turned to my leaders and captains saying, "We will go to our positions in one hour. They will not attack us probably before light." The meeting was ended.

After the Thespian and Theban leaders left, I looked at my captains who were now standing around my fire. I detected that they were in no hurry to end this meeting. I knew, as well as they did, that this is most likely the last time we will ever stand face-to-face.

I looked into the eyes of each of these brave men. Holding my emotion in check, I addressed these Spartan warriors. "Going into battle with you today, I am honored beyond words. Today, Sparta and Greece will lose six of their finest Captains."

In order to maintain our laconic emotional dignity, I could say no more. Spartans do not show tears. But in the cool morning air, the light of my fire showed what could not be concealed. I gave each captain a strong embrace as I whispered the words, "Thank you, my friend." The embrace was returned with silence. No more words were spoken as the captains quietly departed my camp.

I told Sari that if he was going to stay, the least he could do was to feed us a last meal.

Sari and I dined in silence, and then I asked him to help me with my armor.

I faced Sari and had both hands on his shoulders and said, "If you must fight, stay in the rear."

He said back to me, "Why, because you don't think I can fight well?"

I said, "No, it is because I cannot bear to see you fall."

Sari helped me to armor up, and he accompanied me to the wall. When we arrived there, Senri was busy providing some armor to the helots who had decided to stay.

It would be getting light soon, and I thought we should get ready. I went to the top of the wall and noticed that our forward guard now was all Spartans. The rest of the Spartans were gathered behind the wall in a loose formation and resting.

I looked farther behind me to see the Thespians marching up toward us in a phalanx formation.

Gelon joined me on the wall. I told Gelon to send a runner to bring up the rest of the captains and to recover the guards from in front of the wall, so they may join our phalanx.

I looked up over the still dark battlefield and waited. The captains, one-by-one, climbed the ladder.

I spoke to them stating, "The Spartans will lead the phalanx with sixty across followed by the Thespians and helots. You Captains will be in the front line with me. We will make it clear who we are, and we will wear cross-haired helmets in this battle. As soon as it becomes light, we will take the field, as usual, to create the illusion that nothing has changed in our camp." I dismissed my captains to exchange their helmets.

We were minutes from taking the field. I climbed down off the wall and walked over to the Spartans and waited for the captains to arrive with their cross-haired helmets.

While I waited, I received a runner from the East Gate advising me that the Thebans and Thespians were in position.

The field that had once supported the camp of our army was now empty.

The Thespians came to rest. When my captains returned, I told Zee to inform the Thespians of their position in the phalanx. I instructed Senri to inform the helots to where they would fight.

The Thespians had grown used to Zee's commands and immediately changed their formation following his instructions. The Spartans took up their positions at the front of the phalanx.

I ordered, "Phalanx, READY" with my leaders in the front and middle of the formation, leaving me a spot. I ordered them to move forward through the gate. We went through the gate in about six across, and once completely through the gate, we re-formed to our sixty across.

We were unable to fit this phalanx on the field without moving forward of our normal starting position. Because of this, I advanced the first forty across up to a point where we could accommodate the next twenty across. Once this maneuver was complete, I brought the phalanx to rest with helmets up and shields down.

I went out to the front and turned to address the phalanx. I said in a loud voice that seemed to echo in the early morning air. Today's message seemed to be louder resounding against the now familiar sheer mountain cliffs as well as the rebuilt Phocian Wall. "Today the Spartans will lead you into battle, but we are all Greeks, and this is a stand we are making for Greece. Your orders of the day: remain in the phalanx, never stop fighting!"

I said no more and went back and took my position in the phalanx. To my left was Dien and to my right was Gelon. After glancing up and down the line, I noticed some of the Spartan horse-hair plumes were missing or damaged due to the harsh battle conditions of the previous days.

As if on cue, as the sun rose, a rider approached our phalanx and stopped at approximately fifty feet away. He asked for Leonidas.

I stepped forward five steps and said, "I am Leonidas."

The emissary said, "Our great king offers you one final opportunity to lay down your weapons. What is your answer?"

I looked back at my men and then back at the emissary. I said in a voice that reverberated against the rock walls, "Come and take them!"

The emissary waited no longer and rode off immediately.

I turned back to my men to rejoin the phalanx. As I did this, the phalanx came to attention and offered me a salute.

I stopped, looked at the men, and saluted back. I then rejoined the phalanx and waited. We waited at rest.

The activity at the West Gate grew louder as their emissary returned back to their camp. Once again, it was hard to see what was happening so far away. But as the morning got brighter, we could see groups of men forming up closing the distance between us. We could also see the platform that housed Xerxes being moved closer.

My instincts told me that this would be an all-out attack and to expect any weaponry or combination of weaponry that Xerxes possessed.

While we were waiting, the runner I had sent to the Phocian camp arrived back asking me to meet with him. I left the phalanx and met the runner at the gate.

He was breathless but was able to get out the words, "The Persians have gone past the Phocians and are marching toward Alpeni." He estimated that they were approximately one hour behind him and marching at a rapid pace.

I thanked the runner. "Tell the Thespian and Theban leaders what you have learned; then, armor up and rejoin our phalanx. I am sure I can find a place for you here."

He nodded his understanding and left.

I returned to my phalanx, went before the group, and reported to them what I had just learned. I announced to them, "We will soon be cut off!"

I rejoined the phalanx and noticed that the Persians had closed to approximately one-quarter of a mile. Today, they seemed more bunched together than normal. I imagined that Xerxes had probably made enough examples by killing unsuccessful attackers and that failure was not an option.

I ordered the men, "Phalanx, READY."

I then decided, *Why wait any longer realizing that defending our flank was of little consequence?*

I ordered, "Phalanx, FORWARD."

It was not a large phalanx, sixty across and ten to eleven deep, but this was now an experienced phalanx. We marched out with the phalanx now exposed on both the left and right flanks.

The enemy was conditioned to us standing our ground in the narrow portion of the Pass near the Middle Gate. So, our forward movement had to cause some questions. We had now advanced to within one hundred feet of the enemy, and I saw no sign of archers or javelin throwers. The troops we were facing looked as though they were fresh and had not yet seen battle here at Thermopylae.

I then ordered, "All, SPEARS" while we continued to move forward. I gave the order to close the phalanx by tightening its ranks, and we slowed as we first engaged the enemy.

I don't think they were prepared for this thrust of power and the killing that occurred at the ends of our spears. We plowed through one line of men after another walking over the dead and killing the wounded as we went. We were leaving a path of destruction sixty men wide.

This tactic was killing many Persians but was totally leaving our flanks exposed. I decided to take care of one flank by abruptly turning our phalanx ninety degrees to the left and marching toward the mountain. This killing was easier than the first attack due to the fact that these fighters we were now killing, were being surprised. They were not facing us as we attacked them. This caused their spearmen even heavier losses.

We were taking casualties on our flanks and now on our rear as we steadily advanced toward the mountain.

Anywhere we turned the phalanx, we were successful in killing the enemy.

When we got close to the mountain, I called for an about-face of the phalanx. We, once again, began moving forward, this time toward the sea. We were still taking casualties but doing more killing by attacking unsuspecting Persians.

At some point in this battle, the Persians finally understood that we were going to march among them in formation, randomly turning and would continue to kill them.

I then noticed to my left that Xerxes's platform was clearly visible less than a quarter-mile away. I immediately halted the phalanx, turned it back in the direction of Xerxes's platform and ordered the attack to continue.

Our men were reaching an exhaustive level, and I noticed that our flanks had weakened tremendously. A quick glance up and down our lines showed where many Spartans had fallen and were being replaced by Thespians. I also noticed there were only four cross-haired helmets visible to me, but we kept moving.

Before we got within one hundred yards of Xerxes's platform, our phalanx slowed. I realized I had pushed the men as far as they could go. I ordered, "Phalanx, HALT."

We were beginning to take heavy losses as I looked over my shoulder. I also noticed that the left and right flanks had deteriorated with the men on those flanks having to turn to face the enemy. They could no longer maintain the integrity of the phalanx.

What had started out as a little over six hundred men was now down to less than three hundred. I had no new orders to give, so we stood in position. We were being attacked now from all four sides but had taken thousands of the enemy with us. Our men were falling, and I could do nothing to stop it.

I heard a groan beside me, and Gelon went down with a spear in his abdomen. I noticed he had a shocked expression on his face.

As many of our spears were now broken, I turned with my sword to continue to fight. I now realized why the phalanx was falling apart. We were now missing our endless supply of spears.

The battle was raging around me. Screams of both enemy and friend could be heard.

I felt a pain in my leg causing me to drop to one knee. My shield was pushed back against me so far that it knocked my helmet off, and I felt three painful thrusts to my body. I went to the ground unable to move lying face down. That is all I remembered of that moment, but I sensed that I was still at the battle.

I was no longer able to fight but suddenly found myself up on the rocks overlooking the battlefield. I was separated from the battle and its sounds by some unknown transparent barrier. The battle was raging in front of me. I could see it, but I could not hear it. I was calm. I was no longer wearing armor. I felt no pain and my lungs were no longer burning from the exhaustion of the battle. I did not know or understand what was happening, but I was calm. Where I had fallen, the fighting was fiercest.

After a while, it became evident that it was *me* that they were fighting over. The Spartans won the fight for my body costing them even more casualties in doing so. The remaining troops fought their way back to the Phocian Wall.

As they moved closer to the Phocian Wall, my view was expanded to this area. I was still unable to hear anything. It was very quiet where I was. I was very calm and relaxed while observing the events unfold.

As the battle moved, I moved with it. The troops who had rescued me were Spartans and a couple of Thespians.

They carried my body through the gate but were being pursued by the Persians. Once they got through the gate, they took my body over to where I had camped looking for somewhere that could be a defendable position.

I noticed that only a couple of them were carrying spears, some swords, and some, no weapons at all. I could see there were between forty and sixty men who had taken up position on a small hill near where I camped.

The Persians pursued the small force through the Middle Gate. As this occurred, the Immortals appeared from the direction of the East Gate. I saw no sign of the Thespians or Thebans as the Immortals marched toward where we had once camped.

My emotions were calm with the reality that this last group of men had worked so hard just to retain my corpse. The feeling I had was not a sad feeling. It was a feeling of understanding. At that moment, I thought of how ironic it is to finally feel that *I am worthy of being a King.*

I watched as the Persian troops rapidly surrounded the small band of Greeks. The stage was set. I saw one cross-crested helmet as I looked on.

An emissary rode up to the group and offered them their lives if they would surrender the body of the king.

Dien spoke for the group. Although I could not hear the sounds of the battle, I could hear Dien's words clearly, "We stand with our King. We stand with Leonidas."

At this point, Persian archers stepped forward and were stationed on three sides of the Greeks. They were at very close range, less than one hundred feet. Volley after volley of arrows flew, and the Greek force fell one-by-one.

Then there was silence in my realm. My perception was that there was now silence on the battlefield; I was certain of this for the first time in days.

It occurred to me that there were no Greeks alive to bear witness to what had happened here on this final day. None of my brothers from Greece could tell of this heroic stand.

Suddenly, I was no longer able to maintain my view of this scene. I was being drawn somewhere. I still was feeling confusion, but it was a peaceful confusion.

I soon found myself among my fellow Spartans. My Spartans were also within this realm and also without armor appearing calm and at peace. We all shared the same fate with no one life being any more important than the next.

EPILOGUE

I, Leonidas, have moved on since that time and learned through time. After my earthbound life, I learned the true significance of the events of Thermopylae. When you leave your earth body, you do not cease to exist, grow, or learn.

The events of those days transcend way beyond the borders of Greece. Had Persia not eventually been defeated, the world, quite possibly, would not know democratic freedom or democracy. We were defending a way of existing outside of tyranny that impacted the world.

The story I presented is only as complete as my observations and interpretations of the events that I put forth. For many, this will simply be an exciting story about a horrific battle. But to me, the "300" Spartans and the rest of the Greeks who gave their lives are still being honored today for events that happened in 480 BC.

Although the details may be of interest, they are not as important as the reason that this battle was fought. So, arguments concerning the details become irrelevant because the main facts cannot be refuted. The fact is, few stood against many and bought time for the rest to succeed. Those who stayed for the last phalanx paid homage to the words: *honor, integrity,* and *indomitable spirit.*

Pass the story of Thermopylae on to others because no matter whose version of this story you tell, the basic facts remain the same. Through life, people take positive stands that are small and seemingly unimportant while others take stands that are well known and affect many. All of these positive actions strive for equality, justice, and freedom. Perhaps this story will inspire those who wish to take a stand.

ABOUT THE AUTHOR

Alan Bristor, now pursuing his passion for writing, spent time in Greece while serving in the U.S. Army. While there, he became familiar with the well-known mountainous terrain of that country.

He also became aware of the importance of ancient Greek history while attending college. The detailed stories from his professor intensified his interest in this important subject, especially concentrating on the Battle of Thermopylae in 480 BC. This book is the result of Alan's journey to find out about the events surrounding King Leonidas and the 300 Spartans. His perceptions and understanding of these historical events helped to create this riveting story.

As an interesting note, Alan developed his own personal methods of meditation and self-hypnosis through practice, which are now an integral part of the writing process for him.

He is also an accomplished master-level black belt in martial arts and has developed his own fighting system. In addition to authoring books, Alan is a singer-songwriter. He currently resides with his wife in the beautiful Shenandoah Valley in Virginia, known to the locals as the "dimple of the universe."

You can email him at alanbristorsvision@hughes.net.

Made in the USA
Middletown, DE
18 October 2016